ONE MAN'S DESIRE

By

LAREDEAUX

One Man's Desire

Copyright © 2012 LaRedeaux

ISBN-13: 978-0615697772
ISBN-10: 0615697771

This is a work of fiction. Names, characters, businesses, places, events and incidents are either the products of the author's imagination or used in a fictitious manner. Any resemblance to actual persons, living or dead, or actual events is purely coincidental.

Published by Midnight Publications

Written by: LaRedeaux

ACKNOWLEDGEMENTS

Share a smile; it is the key to fit everybody's heart!

Thank you to everyone that encouraged me along this journey.

To my Family thanks for all you do.

Dedicated to my #1 **kisses**

ONE MAN'S DESIRE

Midnight
PUBLICATIONS

Hilton Speaks....

One Man's Journal

Taking the recommendation of his therapist, Hilton decided to stop into Staples while heading home. He felt extremely odd in the store looking for a journal. After all, it seemed like something women were into.

My life is a mess. First my wife won't make love to me, I am seeing a therapist, and now I have to keep my thoughts on paper in a freaking journal.

Wow, he thought shaking his head, to release some of the tension that was building.

There have been so many things he wanted to do lately that, Marie was still unable or unwilling to do. He wanted to talk to Chase more, but he already knew exactly what he would say. Their conversations rang in his mind clearly. He refused to acknowledge the desire constantly building in him, even though the pressure sometimes seemed unbearable. Women constantly throwing themselves at him were an issue that he was unsure he would be able to withstand much longer.

Picking up a couple of items, he made his way towards the stationary section. Browsing through the countless number of notebooks and journals available, his eyes landed on a camel colored leather book. Picking it up, he fingered the intricately embossed design, gracing the cover that made it look regal and unlike a diary, or the many other journals gracing the shelf. Untying the leather cord, he flipped it open, staring at the blank pages.

Nothing beats a failure, but a try.

Hilton placed the journal in his cart and headed towards the check out. There were so many things going through his mind that, he needed an avenue of release before he released *something else*.

Day one....

In all honesty, I don't know what to put down in this book. Writing in a journal should be something Dr. Jeffers

recommends to her female clientele only. I
am not really sure if this journaling thing is
for me, but I have to try, or my marriage
may be in serious danger. There is no time
like the present so here goes...

I attended my last session with Dr.
Jeffers and my wife today. Marie was
reluctant to go as usual, but after informing
her that this was supposed to be our last
session, she agreed. She sat, stiff looking, as
if she would rather be anywhere else. Dr.
Jeffers told us we could each continue our
individual sessions and we were making
some progress.

Clearing his throat, Doctor Jeffers said,
"A marriage is like a three strand cord, it is
intertwined with: Man, Woman and God.
In order for it to remain successful, you
have to continue to learn and grow as a
couple. Aside from God, there is nothing
more important than the vows you made to
each other. Children, family and business
fall behind the role of husband and wife."

These women are coming to work out dressed like they are going to the club. Why am I being tortured so damn much? I swear if another woman comes on to me today, I am going to take her into my office and fuck her on top of my desk.

Day four...

4:30 a.m.

The last two days have been extremely busy. I am truly thankful for days like those. It lets me get my main focus back on track. Sometimes when I am feeling weak, I want to just do things I know would compromise everything I have worked so hard for. Guilt is a heavy burden to bear! The thoughts that ran through my head constantly over the past couple days, has me feeling a certain kind of way. My other head is doing a lot of thinking right now. I guess I better get to working out and release some tensions.

2:00 p.m.

I'm going to try and catch up with Chase. I called Marie to have lunch with her today and she's too busy. It seems like she never has the time for me anymore. Work, the kids, and her "me time" takes precedence over me. These excuses are really driving me over the edge. If I fall, I may never get back up again.

Damn, I can't seem to get this stuff off my mind. Chase is busy doing personal training sessions and my wife won't give me the time of day. I can't win for losing. Guess I'll drive around for a bit, maybe walk through the mall. For now, I guess I'll get back to work, check out some of my trainers and make sure they are holding things down.

Day five...

10:30 am

I am truly blessed and business is good. The accountant just left our monthly meeting, announcing the figures for the fiscal year's end report and I couldn't be happier. There has been a surge in enrollments during the last six months, thanks to my managers implementing the easy sign-up procedures we discussed. The payment plans for membership have almost doubled the total number of members. I am so glad I followed that suggestion. I feel like celebrating with the love of my life. I have given all the employees a decent bonus this month and I am sure most of them will be surprised come Friday. Only one manager knows about the bonuses, because he handles the newsletters.

5:00 p.m.

It hurts to love someone with all your being and not have that love returned. I am lost at what to do. Instead of having dinner with my lovely wife, I am sitting in the damn parking lot. I called her at noon to tell her the great news and to tell her I wanted to go out and celebrate tonight. She seemed happy at first, until Cole walked in saying he needed her to stay over and complete a damn report. I swear I don't like that dude. I keep asking her to quit that fucking job and she says she didn't get a master's degree to sit at home. I just don't fucking understand these independent woman issues. She owns half of our business. I made sure of that, because I purchased it myself from Chase. What the hell is going on with her? I've overheard plenty of women say that, they want a man like me. Why doesn't my wife want me?

Day six...

4:30 a.m.

Pastor McClendon scared the living shit out of me last night. Dude really moves in silence. I didn't even see him when he walked up on my truck. He tapped on the window and I nearly jumped out of the seat. I was so caught up in my own feelings. I will have to pay him back for that shit. After he finished laughing at my ass, he convinced me to come to bible study.

I feel so enlightened now. I know I can finish this fight and I will have my wife again. I won't give up on the vows I made. I love her more than the air I breathe. I just have to find a way to reach her again. The spark has died, but I swear on my life, I am going to relight that flame.

Pastor McClendon hit hard last night! I haven't been to bible study in a couple of months. But last night, he reaffirmed my belief. I can still hear his voice echoing in my head....

"Malachi 3:10: Test me in this, says the Lord Almighty. Every man has a right to put his hand upon God's promises as his own. Every person can put the promises to the test. God is not a man that he can tell a lie. When he speaks a truth, it is so."

I believe that word was for me. I sat questioning God and myself last night. Now I know that, what is meant for me is mine. Nothing can take that away. Thank you Pastor

I know my today is going to be greater than yesterday.

1:00 p.m.

I have been busy as heck today. I made breakfast for Marie and the kids this morning before leaving for work. I know she loves eggs Florentine and the kids love my chocolate waffles. I placed a note on her tray beside the bed, kissing her forehead before heading to the gym. This morning was my first day, with a special set of women and men who entered our weight management course. I hired a personal nutritionist to develop meal plans for each individual client. I, along with two of my personal trainers set their workout schedules. This group had to have special attention, because they were at least one hundred pounds over their target weight. Half of them are cigarette smokers and that alone takes a lot of work. Thankfully, my newest trainer is an ex-Newport cigarette fanatic and learned a great strategy for anyone trying to quit smoking. I am skeptical about two of the women and one of the men. I don't believe they will last, because they were reluctant to sign up for the smoke cessation program. One thing is for sure, you can lead a horse to water, but you can't make him drink or not puff.

I don't have any clients scheduled this afternoon. I am going to make an early day and head home, pick up the kids, and hopefully get some quality time in with

Marie. I pray that she will at least let me hold her tonight.

I think I'll swing by Pink House on the way home, pick up flowers and Tony Roma's for some ribs. Yeah that's it dinner and flowers tonight should be good. If I take away some of the household duties, it should help take away the attitude and melt the ice. Damn, it's been cold at my house.

Day seven...

4:30 am

When in the hell did she stop eating pork? I can't understand this shit; it is getting worse by the day. She stared at the ribs like it was the fucking black plague. I know she has been eating lighter since J.J. was born, but shit she just made pork chops a few months ago. They were broiled I remember. J.J. whined because he wanted chicken nuggets and we disagreed on that.

Did she even eat that night? Think Hill...when did she stop eating pork. Fuck it; I know she still eats pork. I made her breakfast with eggs Florentine and bacon. She thanked me for breakfast when I called and she ain't mention shit about not eating the bacon. That shit is pork! Just another wasted attempt, why is this shit so hard? I know marriage isn't all peaches and cream, but damn, I am trying as hard as I can. I wonder if I got with someone else would that even matter.

Day eight....

4:30 am

I didn't go home last night and Marie didn't even care. She called me at midnight saying the kids were going to her mom's house for the weekend. She didn't even bother to ask if I was coming in. Shit, she didn't even bother to ask about my day or anything. Other than informing me, she would be working on Saturday that was our conversation. These Saturday hours have become a regular occurrence. The kids don't mind, because her mother spoils them, just like mine does. We have some great parents. But damn, what about me, I mind! I hate that she thinks of this job more than she does me and I'm tired.

2:00 p.m.

All my clients have been serviced. My calendar is free for the rest of the day and late into tomorrow. I could go home, but who wants to go to an empty house. I could go catch a movie, or stop by and holla at Chase. Naw, it's Friday night and I'm pretty sure he has a date tonight. So a movie it is. Hopefully something good is playing I need a good laugh.

Day nine...

4:30 am

Today is not looking like a good day. Dear God, please come and take this pain away. I don't want to feel this way in my heart. Help me, please

8:00 am

I tried to kiss Marie and she turned her head. I didn't want an argument, just a damn kiss. It's a horrible feeling, not to know what is going on in her mind. I feel like giving up, because this shouldn't really be that hard.

1:00 pm

I felt so bad about our argument this morning, I decided to take her flowers and ask her out to lunch. What a big mistake that was. She barely smiled, when she said she couldn't go to lunch. As I walked out of her office, her assistant offered to take me to lunch. I don't get it...even her assistant wants to spend time with me, but not my own wife.

I called Desiree', asked her if she had time to eat today and she accepted. This woman is wonderful. She runs her own business from home, but she makes time for me. I will cherish the friendship we have forever. She is giving me what I need from my wife. She listens to me talk about Marie, without judgment. I don't understand why she won't start dating again. She says she's fine, but I know her ex-husband really did a number on her. Maybe I should introduce her to Chase. He could really use a strong woman in his corner.

Day twenty...

4:30 a.m.

Waking up with purpose for the last two weeks, I had forgotten to make any entries. Well, after spending the day with Desiree' we really became closer. She laughs at my jokes, listens to me talk, and doesn't complain about a damn thing. I thought about introducing her to Chase, but that is not about to happen. My feelings have grown so much for her in the last two weeks. I can't see anyone with her, least of all Chase. I feel rejuvenated in her company. And those eyes, I can get lost in them. When she smiles, awe my heart just flip flops. I know that she is feeling me, maybe not in the same way, but I know I am growing on her. Our vibe is just in sync.

Last week I told her about my impending anniversary. It Seems like I always end up talking about Marie and she just listens, not uttering one single, negative word in response. I don't think many women would do that. She's a different kinda woman, that's for sure.

What's happening in My Home?

Standing in the mirror admiring his smooth chocolate skin, Hilton decided that no longer would he spend endless nights dreaming about making love to the woman of his desire. Tonight, he would make his move. He would show her just how much his desire had grown for her. He shared a life without sexual fulfillment with his wife and that only made his yearning for Desiree' grow more.

Reminiscing about last night, he couldn't help but wonder what really is going on with his wife.

Is my wife secretly seeing someone else, has she grown tired of me, do I not satisfy her anymore?

Shaking the thoughts out of his head, Hilton looked back at his lovely Marie. She was still sleeping beautiful and peacefully. Although they had been married for more than twelve years and had two beautiful children, Hilton still felt lucky to be married to her. From the moment they met more than fifteen years ago, he had been helplessly in love with her. June 5 1997, was a day he'd never forget.

Stopping off to grab a quick energy fix while en-route to his shop, he met the most beautiful woman he had ever seen. Her smile was like sunshine on a cloudy day. Being the gentleman he was, gawking was not necessary. He smiled and paid for her drink along with his. Standing there looking like a ray of sunshine, dressed in a yellow lined dress that accented her round ass and perky breast, she was breathtaking. And twelve years and two children later, she still made his heart skip a beat.

Hilton snapped out of the past. He knew those days were long over. Last night, for the millionth time in five years, the love of his life rejected him once again. He could not understand why nothing he tried worked, but last night was his last straw.

Being the faithful devoted husband would be a thing of the past. As he reminisced about last night, and how perfect it would have been to make love to his wife again, he grew angry. Thinking of all the effort and preparation he put into the night made him silently weep at the rejection he felt. The week began with lilies being sent to her at work, which is not unusual since he did that often, but the note he attached to the flowers was an indicator of what was to come.

"*To my beautiful wife of twelve years, I have loved you from the moment we laid eyes on each other. Every time I close my eyes, I see your beautiful face. When I wake in the morning I know that God loves me so much, because I am able to see your beautiful smile. I reach out to touch my dream and its really lying next to me. My love for you has never changed. I love you more than the breath I breathe. You are the Angel that God let me borrow. I love you, Hilton*"

The next day, he decided to send her two dozen berries from one of her favorite sites. It was her guilty indulgence, chocolate strawberries dipped in white and dark chocolate. Hilton knew the winning combination of chocolate and strawberries was an aphrodisiac to many, him included. He adored feeding her the sexual berries. The way she held her mouth when taking a bite out of the luscious fruit, always sent waves through his body. Although she would never eat more than four of the delectable berries, she thoroughly enjoyed the treat and always shared with the other females in the office who rarely got anything. Tuesday's note was based on his passion.

"To my exotic wife, as you indulge in this sweet treat, I am reminded of the first time we made love. That night was the most wonderful night of my life. I can still taste your sweetness on my tongue. Smell the sweet fragrant musk of your perfume and feel the silkiness of your body as we became one for the very first time. It was the night I floated to heaven and thanked God for giving me you. That very same night I asked you to be mine; forever. I was addicted to your sweet loving. You are my Angel and I love you, Hilton."

He had lunch delivered on Wednesday by her favorite restaurant *Ruth Chris*. He made sure it was enough to feed the entire office. He attached a note to the special lunch of Lobster Florentine just for her. Thursday was lingerie from Victoria Secret. She still loved to wear frilly things to bed. He preferred Adam and Eve, but she rarely wares those items. The silky pieces were accompanied by three carat VVS stones, set in platinum to caress her ears. Friday he chose to have her serenade by a local musician, who did perfect renditions of Will Downing's, *Riding on a Cloud*. It was both of their favorite songs. The day ended with a limo ride to her favorite day spa, where she could enjoy a full afternoon experience of relaxation and pampering.

Hilton knew in his heart she would not deny him the pleasure of making love to her once again. How long could a man wait to make love to his wife? There was no physical or mental reason he could muster up. Everything had been executed perfectly. He felt there was no way possible for her to deny him, *again*. The children, Aryssa who was entering her pre-teen years and J.J. who was five going on fifty, were away at their grandparent's house for the weekend. The house was lit with candles, roses and soft music playing throughout. Their massive California king bed was freshly made with crisp new 1500 count Egyptian sheets. The room was completely redone today as a final surprise.

There should have been no reason for her not to make love to me.

Glancing over his shoulder once again, he realized how wrong he was.

4:30 a.m.

Journal Entry

Last night was such a disaster. Why does everything have to go so terribly wrong? I know that spending so much time with Desiree' isn't a good idea, but she has lit a fire in me that is just bursting to get out. Everything I planned for this week had been executed perfectly and last night was supposed to be the icing on the cake. It's not supposed to be this way. I should be making love to my wife right now. Well, since she doesn't want me it's time to find someone who does. My needs will soon be fulfilled.

Walking back in front of the mirror silently weeping and reminiscing over the painful thoughts of his denial, Hilton decided he would no longer wait to appease his manhood.

At that very moment, his desire changed and his manhood grew and throbbed uncontrollably. Smiling and wiping the remaining tears from his eyes, Hilton decided it was time to call her bluff. While Hilton continued to get dressed, he could barely contain himself.

"Many nights he was alone, many, many nights his light was too bright...."

He started to hum lyrics of one of Desiree's favorite songs by Erykah Badu, *Orange Moon*. He couldn't seem to get the tunes from Desire's iPod playlist out his mind. She was the exact opposite of his wife, yet she had captivated him in so many ways. Hilton knew he had to have her. Yet, due to his status she would not relent. He was very attracted to her, even though she down played her beauty.

Desire' was a thick sistah standing at 5'5", with breast a size 42DD, her waist was thick and she had an ass that made his dick raise every time she walked by. She was very unpretentious and sexy at the same time. She had long natural black hair that, she recently colored to a soft chocolate brown. Her eyes were green, yet she wore colored contacts. He remembered her saying she didn't like her eyes, because they reminded her of her mother's green eyes. Her light caramel reflection made those contacts look so natural that many people thought that they were.

Hilton remembered the first time he met Desire', she had cried on his shoulder three years ago on the night of her anniversary. That day she told him how she finally came to realize her marriage was completely over. Although Hilton encouraged her to give the man another chance, Desire' was fed up. She confessed to being in a doomed marriage with a man who refused to give her the one thing he gave everyone else, his love. Desire' didn't have children yet; her husband had several that she cared for dearly. After nearly three hours of talking about her husband, Hilton finally got a smile out of Desire'. When he began to sing Will Downing's *A Million Ways* to her, her smile was an eclipse on his heart. She confessed Will was her favorite male artist, because of his silky voice. That night Desire' would not let him leave without feeding him for his time. She prepared his favorite meal, smothered pork chops, mashed red potatoes and homemade cream corn and cornbread all from scratch. He hadn't had his favorite dish in so long that he physically licked the plate clean. That was the beginning of a friendship he wanted to continue. However, his current state left him wanting more and more. Desire' unknowingly had become his untimely desire.

Stepping out to his 2010 Ford Explorer, Hilton felt that tonight, he would tell Desire' just how much he wanted her? Tonight, would be the night when he laid things on the line. Since it had been five years since he made love to his wife, he prayed he could convince Desire' to love him at least one time. No matter what the cost he would have his Desire fulfilled.

***

Desire' couldn't believe all the lavish attention Hilton was giving her. She was constantly receiving something from him. Today it was book gift basket with some her favorite authors inside; Rochelle Alers,

Vanessa Davis Griggs, Wahida Clark, Treasure Blue and Envy Red. It also contained videos, chocolates and Will Downing's new Anthology along with a bottle of her favorite Moscato wine. She had come to realize their friendship was gradually changing. The text messages had gotten a lot more intense and the daily calls were more frequent. The attraction wasn't his entire fault, or a one way. Desire' had to admit she was mutually attracted to Hilton, but continued to remind herself he was off limits.

Since her divorce, Desire' had remained celibate. She didn't fully trust men any longer and found she was much happier single. That is, until now. She stood in her full length mirror admiring the dress Hilton delivered to her yesterday. She just couldn't understand or believe if he was telling the truth about not sleeping with the wife he loved for the last five years. She was beginning to think maybe she should entertain the thought giving him this Desire' he yearned for.

Placing the finishing touches on her hair, Desire' decided that tonight's menu would be her. She placed the dress on the bed. Thinking about Hilton made her creamy and moist. She began to wonder if sex with Hilton was going to be as good as her day dreams.

As Desire' submitted to the thoughts of having Hilton as her lover, she was overwhelmed with emotion. When her clitoris began to throb uncontrollably, she knew she had to release the tension before Hilton arrived, or she would be standing naked in the doorway.

Deciding how to approach this situation was going to be a task, Desire' silently thought as she showered. She knew this would be playing with fire.

What if it all went horribly wrong? What if I misread the signals I thought Hilton was sending?

Being a bit shy and somewhat of a country girl, she could very well be taking his kindness in the wrong way. Before leaving the shower, she decided she would just wait for Hilton to make the first move. It would be better to talk things out before moving into something she had never done before, like having an affair.

***

Driving down the parkway, Hilton decided it might be better to text Desire' instead of calling. Maybe this way, he could truly tell her how much he had come to want and need her in his life. The advances he was making didn't seem to be going as fast as he would like. His lower head was thinking for him 99% of the time lately, but now he was thinking with his brain and heart.

"Desire', babe I know that we have been skirting around some very big issues. But I can no longer contain myself. These past few weeks have meant more to me than you can ever realize. You have made me feel like a man in more ways than one. Although I know you're not open to being in a relationship with me due to my situation, I promise you that I have decided to end that if you will have me. I can't think of anyway else. I can't think of anyone else. I've tried everything that a man can. I even took your suggestion. Nothing worked, this man is tired and is ready to be a man again, and I want to be that man with you, H."

As he pressed send, Hilton breathed a sigh of relief and smiled. Feeling like things were finally headed in a promising direction, Hilton decided to make a quick stop at his favorite florist to bring Desire' her favorite flowers. He smiled at the thought of the reaction he would get when presenting her with radiant red long stem roses, along with pretty in pink Asiatic lilies in a beautiful crystal vase. With all his stops complete, Hilton merged into traffic en-route to his Desire'.

***

Standing in the kitchen, hopelessly gazing out the window, Desire' watched as the gorgeous sunny day drifted off into a sudden spray of dark clouds accompanied by thunder and lightning. The sudden change in weather marked Desire's sudden change in her mood. She quickly left the kitchen and headed to her ringing cell phone and retrieved a message from Hilton.

"Desire', I will be arriving in forty-five minutes and I can't wait to see you."

With that message, Desire' decided to give Hilton a greeting he would never forget.

Changing into something sexy would definitely put her on the menu. As she scanned through her lingerie, her eyes landed on a piece that would surely make any many rock hard. Grabbing her cell Desire' sent Hilton a message to let him know she was ready for his arrival.

"Hi, I can't wait to see you too. The Front Door is open and I'll be waiting."

***

As Hilton pulled into the parking space, Desire' could hear him playing Will's new anthology *Sexy,* a song that would surely be a hit if it could get some airplay. Quickly grabbing her IPod, she set the song to play through her sound system, so that when he entered it could continue.

As Hilton opened the door, he could hear Will's silky smooth voice singing.

"Touch me, feel me, hold me, Sexy, sexy baby can you do that for me...."

Smiling he looked down at the flowers, he cradled in his hands. He nearly dropped the bouquet at the sight of Desire'. He thought his eyes were going to pop out of his head, while standing there with his mouth wide open staring at Desire'.

She is so full of surprises.

Not able to take his eyes off her, slowly she walked over to him smiling. Gazing at her from head to toe, he noticed she displayed a sexy confidence, radiating from within. Seeing her standing before him, in such a way brought his dick fully to life without a single touch. He could barely contain himself as she spoke to him.

"Hi Hilton, I'm so happy to see you. Are those beautiful roses for me?"

"D...D...Desire' you are breathtaking, yes these are for you."

"Why are you stuttering?"

"I have never seen you look so beautiful," Hilton said. "Of course you always have been beautiful to me, but right now you're making me stutter."

"Can I have my flowers, so that we can begin dinner?" Desire' asked, while reaching out her hands. She was careful not to get too close to Hilton.

Realizing that his manhood was on display he said, "My Desire', let me place these over here." Hilton quickly responded.

When Desire' turned around to head towards the kitchen, he thought he was losing his mind and eye sight. He couldn't stop staring or blinking. Here she was walking into the kitchen wearing a barely noticeable G-string that displayed her full round ass. That ass seemed to call out his name. He was still in shock as she turned to him holding a glass. He was aware of the motion of her lips, but could not hear the words coming out of her mouth. His eyes roamed her body; she had the complete set up on. The sheer silky fabric of the fuchsia and black lingerie she wore was shaped like an apron. Her big breasts sat upright in the pink and black trimmed fabric. They beaconed to him as he could see her fully erect nipples. The sleek fabric that led down her stomach did not hide the shapely curves as her regular clothing did. Hilton was completely mesmerized, as he stood there looking at her. Her mouth was moving, as she began walking back towards him. The bottom of the apron lingerie swayed as her hips moved, it also was the same hot fuchsia color as the top. While he stood there gazing at her, she continued to talk to him yet, he could not hear anything that she said. He was busy taking in all the beauty that was before him.

"Hilton...Hilton." Desire' said, interrupting his reverie, "would you like a glass of JC and Coke, or would you like some of my wine?"

Snapping out of his daze, he was finally able to mutter a word, "Yes dear, please I'll have some JC and Coke." Hilton said, as his eyes once again focused on her ass.

That G-string seemed to continue whispering his name. "Come find me," he thought he heard it say. As he stood to take the glass from her, he felt beads of sweat forming on his head, as his manhood continued to throb underneath his slacks. He knew that if he didn't do something quick, he would spill his seed all over his pants. Taking the glass and excusing himself, Hilton slowly walked backwards down the hall to the bathroom unable to take his eyes off Desire', until reaching the door behind him. That is when he was finally able to breathe. He let out a strong sigh of relief, which signaled that he had been holding his breath for far too long.

***

Desire' felt her own creamy moistness between her legs, as she stood there watching Hilton retreat to the bathroom. She was very glad he decided to leave the room for a moment. She knew instantly she had not made the wrong choice in attire as

Hilton, who could formulate any sentence eloquently was standing before her stuttering relentlessly. She began to smile at the thought of the things to come during the night. Her thoughts then drifted to the sight of Hilton's engorged manhood demanding his presence be seen. Although he tried to remain composed, she could still see his manhood threatening to burst out of his slacks. She smiled, not believing she had this effect on a man. Her former husband was not the least bit excited when she would strut around in various outfits.

***

Hilton emerged from the bathroom with only one objective in mind and that was to fulfill his Desire'. He came up the hall with movements as swift as a beast in pursuit of its prey. He eyed his target, with the stealth of a cheetah he swept her up in his arms and pulled her into an embrace that would be the first of many. Keeping his eyes on the beauty in his arms, he kissed her, as if it were his last kiss. His eyes were aflame, as their tongues caressed and formed a dance. He kissed her so passionately that their breath mingled as one. The sensations of her wine mixed with his JC, causing him to press his tongue as deep as it would go. He thought he could feel her tonsils as he continued to dance within her mouth.

Time seemed to stand still as Hilton gently pulled back from kissing his Desire'. He gave her rapid sets of short kisses while trailing his tongue around her lips, down her chin and landing on the dead center of her neck. He rotated between sucking and kissing. Hilton could hear Desire' moan his name, "Oh Hilton Ooooh."

His passion grew stronger. He lifted Desire' into his arms and headed for the bedroom where candles burned and music played softly. However, all the music he needed was emitting from Desire's beautiful full lips.

Laying Desire' on the bed, Hilton mounted atop her and just stared at the lovely flecks of brown in her green eyes. He was completely mesmerized by this woman. As his heart began to pound in his chest, his erection suddenly grew. Slow and meticulously he raised the skirt of her apron lingerie. A small gasp escaped his lips, when he saw the most heavenly sight. He had not tasted the sweet nectar of a woman in five years, and looking at her lush body made him swoon.

***

Desire' thought her heart was going to jump out of her chest as Hilton laid her on the bed and began to undress her. She smiled as sweetly as she could, yet she was a nervous wreck on the inside. She was still in awe of what was happening around her. He stood above her gazing down into her eyes. He beamed like a child on Christmas morning.

He began kissing her deeply, as his hands roamed all over her soft body. He was in heaven. It felt as if it had been centuries since he had been able to make love to a woman. Truthfully, at this moment he was in heaven. His lips made their way to her breast. Placing his tongue around the top of her nipple, he slowly traced down to the back and made loops around her hardened pecks. With one breast in hand and one in mouth, Desire' moaned helpless to the suckling of Hilton's mouth. Just when she felt she could no longer keep from screaming, he released her breast and began his descent downwards.

Removing her G-String, he quickly noticed a trimmed pussy that made him devour her quickly. He was truly going to have his way with her tonight. If there was one thing he loved about eating pussy, it was one that was well trimmed. He dove into that pussy like a beast, loving the smell, the taste and the feel of her pussy. It was pure bliss and it felt as though her sweetness captivated him. As he suckled on her clitoris, his hands roamed through to find her opening and at that moment of entry he was hooked.

Desire' felt her body trembling from the moment he first touched her vagina. She could not believe Hilton was ravaging her body this way. It felt as if she was floating on a cloud. She moaned and screamed as he took command of her pussy as no other man had ever done.

"Don't stop, please don't stop. I'm coming." She moaned.

At that very moment, she was addicted. Hilton ate her pussy relentlessly for what seemed like an hour.

Rising, he said, "Tonight, I am just going to eat your pussy all night long. It tastes like sunshine on a cloudy day."

Hilton moaned, because it tasted so good. Desire' didn't know if it was the energy or the stamina. His sucking and licking caused her to have more orgasms. More than she had ever had in her entire sexual life.

She was floating in a whirlwind and never felt such emotions overwhelm her, as they did tonight. It was as if she had been taking into another level of making love. Not in her life had she had so many orgasms without penile penetration. The way he caressed her clitoris with only his mouth, sent her screaming again and again.

"I'm coming, ooh we I'm coming....Oh Hilton."

She could barely keep count of the number of times he made her scream and come. This man certainly knew how to eat a pussy. As she drifted off into slumber with Hilton in her arms, she thought he should teach a pussy eating class. Many men would benefit from that skill. Every part of her body felt contented and exhausted from the wild combinations of positions as Hilton was like a mercenary ravaging her clitoris and vagina. A smile curved her lips as she lay next to her chocolate Adonis.

Desire'

I can't wait to kiss your
Soft and gentle lips,
And wrap my arms around your hips,
To make you moan and call me lover,
To wish our session is never over.
For my kisses to be in
Tune with your heart.
You set me on fire as my legs part,
You make me wet as morning dew,
As I bring out the freak in you!
You make me scream as
You lick my clit.
The pleasure of you
Squeezing my behind,
As the lust overtakes our mind.
As we lay spent from all of our desire

Still warm from our sensual fire.
I will whisper in your ear as
You hold me tight,
Baby I am yours all night!

"Baby, are you awake?" Hilton whispered.

"Yes," said Desire', as she lay there with her eyes closed thinking about what had transpired and what was about to happen now.

"I'd love to watch the sun rise in your eyes, Desire', but I have to go home."

Turning to look at the bedside clock, Desire' realized how late it was.

"Yes I know it's almost four thirty in the morning. What are you going to say when you get home?"

"Don't worry about that, I'm sure Marie doesn't even realize I'm not there." Powering up his phone, he spoke again, "I want to capture this moment just like this, you're even more beautiful than you realize."

Snapping the picture he rose and gathered his clothing that was thrown around the room and headed to the shower. She remained lying in bed with a million thoughts running through her head.

What happens now, where will this go? Will he really leave Marie? Does she really want him too? Could she trust a man again?

Shaking the thoughts out of her mind, she decided to just savor the moment. It had been so long since a man, any man, took interest in her the way he did. So she decided at that moment, to ride the ride while it lasted. Being that they only had oral sex all night, she laid there while he showered, dressed and kissed her goodnight before heading out the door to go home. Soon she was drifting back off to a dreamless peaceful sleep.

THE AFTERMATH

What happens after the morning after, after the night before?

Hilton was still floating when he arrived home. He realized during his ride that he had never been out this late without his wife. He felt no need to make up an excuse figuring that she probably never realized he didn't come home. He never thought there would ever be a time when he didn't love his wife and the life they built together. Yet, after last night he began to really question if she loved him anymore? How could the woman he fell in love with deny him for so many years.

Sitting inside his garage he thought back over the five years he had not been able make love to his wife.

After the first two years of not being able to make love to his wife, they went to marriage counseling. Their marriage was on very shaky ground. Yet, the thought of sleeping with another woman didn't even cross his mind at that time. Funny he thought how things had changed. For that entire year of marriage counseling with the pastor at their church and a professional therapist, there never was a reason given why Marie refused to have sex with him. He thought many times that maybe she was having an affair but quickly dismissed the idea. She loved him. During one of their many sessions, he flat out asked her right in front of the pastor. He didn't know what had come over him when he blurted out the words.

"Marie, are you sleeping with another man, because you damn sure ain't sleeping with me?" Startled at the sound of his own voice he continued. "Marie what is it? What can I do to get you to make love to me once again? I love you! Of course, our marriage isn't based on sex. We have more than that, but I want you to know I need to make love to my wife. To feel like a man, to consummate our love and marriage, I need you to show me and give me physical intimate contact. We have lost that connection."

His pleas landed on deaf ears that night. Standing up she smiled, turned and walked out of the Pastors office. Hilton remembered the look she gave him; he had never seen her smirk like that before. Then she turned and smiled brilliantly at their pastor before strutting out of the door. He stood before his pastor, crying openly. That was the first time he had ever cried before another man. Feeling defeated, he remembered his pastor coming over and saying, "Just be patient son."

Snapping out of his daze, Hilton thought to himself *patience wears thin*. Three years ago he decided to be patient. But now there was no patience left. Last night with Desire' had him nervous and extremely anxious. He knew in his mind that he would never leave his wife. There was no other woman he loved more than Marie. Even with all her constant rejection, he still loved the very ground she walked on.

However, he knew that Desire' could give him everything he was missing at home. He would do his best not to hurt her and give her all that he could, starting with last night.

4:30 a.m.

Journal Entry

Last night was amazing. Desire' tasted like sweet Georgia peaches. I felt like a man again. When she opened the door, I couldn't do anything but gaze at the beauty standing before me. I was blown away, so much that I stuttered. Damn, I hadn't done that in many years. I am going to have to replay my diction exercises, before seeing her again like that. I feel so rejuvenated, almost like fresh water trickling over mountain streams. It's amazing what some good tasting pussy can do for you. I can't wait to see what it feels like when I am inside her tight walls. Damn, let me go pump some iron, because I have to do something with this energy.

***

Running his tongue over his teeth, Hilton remembered how sweet her juices were. She was so wet and creamy he thought. Sitting and thinking about, how good her pussy tasted had his dick rising all over again. Shaking his head, he knew those thoughts would have to wait. He had to get out of the car and head inside to prepare for his busy day. Heading towards his home gym he made a note to himself that he would send an invite to his wife to attend the movies tonight with him and his son. Although he was sure she would decline. He nevertheless made attempts to appease his wife. Tonight, he and J.J. would enjoy the new hit movie *Avengers* that everyone is raving over. He knew that his son was looking forward to the evening.

Inside his home gym Hilton kept reliving the previous night's images. Those images had him pressing and lifting more weight than he had previously done. Three hours later he found himself still sitting inside the gym. Sitting up with sweat dripping down his chiseled abdomen, he removed his now soaked t-shirt and allowed the cool water to drip down his face and chest. Since today was an off day, raising he decided he would go run a few laps over the Tallmadge Bridge before the sun blazing forth.

Walking into the guest bath he quickly changed and headed to his car to complete the 6 am run. Thinking to himself, he'll arrive back home before 8 am when he was sure his wife would be up and getting the kids ready for school, before she left for work.

MARIE

Standing in her mirror looking back at a woman she hardly recognized Marie felt a surge of anger that she just couldn't seem to shake off. She knew that she was to fault for the state of her marriage, however she was completely lost on how to change the circumstances back around. The early years of her marriage had been wonderful. She loved and adored the man who had captured her heart fifteen years ago. Hilton Jacob Scott was the essence of a good black man. They dated and he thoroughly courted her for three years before they married. They shared so many good times. Yet, after giving birth to her son Hilton J.R. something changed for her. She no longer saw Hilton in the same light. He did not change a thing about the way he loved her or cared for their family.

After seeing a therapist, a pastor and her normal physician during the second year after J.J.'s birth, she still felt the same way. Her desire for Hilton had left. At first she thought it was just normal Postpartum Depression. Upon the suggestions of her doctor, they hired a nanny to help care for J.J. during his first six months of life. Marie went back to work and life seemed to become normal once again. However, she still was unable to make love or express love with Hilton.

Finally, after a year of treatment and talks she gave up the fight. She knew depression wasn't her problem and even though she sought the help of a therapist she was still unable to admit to what her therapist said. It was not possible for her to be attracted to anyone else. Marie only had eyes for Hilton ever since the day he paid for her drink at a local Parkers store, while out on a lunchtime break. The words of her therapist rang loud in her head as she stood in the mirror.

"Marie, the problem you are having with Hilton is that, you have become attracted to someone else. This is common in marriages, especially after having children and growing apart. I am sure that you will become attracted to your husband once again. There is no need for you to continue on the Zoloft since your postpartum depression has passed. Take a trip; enjoy some of the luxuries your husband lays at your feet. Many women that I see would kill to have a husband like yours."

Still contemplating that she was attracted to someone else, she shook that thought off as she mentally scanned all the men she came into contact with on a daily basis. It was not possible. She worked in downtown Savannah. There were hundreds of people in and out of her building daily. Her boss was a very handsome man, who after ten years of working with her, still let her know on a daily basis how attracted to her he was. She always dismissed his advances and made it clear that she loved her husband only. Cheating was not an option. Looking at the clock on the bedside table she realized it was time to get the kids off school. Since she had Mondays and Tuesday off, today she decided she would veer off from her normal schedule and do something different.

On the ride back from dropping the kids at school, Marie found herself strolling through Barnes and Nobles on Abercorn. Sifting through sections of books she decided to pick up a couple of books she had never heard of. Heading to the counter with her purchases, she decided her first read would be *Touch* by Envy Red. The cover attracted her to the book and after skimming the back, she knew she would have to read this book. She also picked up *An Accidental Affair by Eric Jerome Dickey*, and *Harlem Girl Lost* by Treasure E. Blue.

Today was going to be a day of relaxation for Marie, or at least that was the plan. Retrieving her cell phone, Marie decided to check her messages before heading to Jalapeno's for lunch.

Pulling out her Galaxy S3, Marie tapped her message app to see what she feels is the usual stuff from Hilton.

"My love good morning, I hope your day is as beautiful as you are too me. I love you always and forever, Hilton."

Storing the messages in the folder marked H. She shrugged it off and went straight to the SMS Backup she stored on both their phones when they arrived over two months ago. Although she never read the messages, she definitely noticed the number and the times they always arrived and were sent. Making a mental note to sit down and print all the messages out she pulled out of Barnes and Noble parking lot and headed to her favorite getaway spot for lunch.

Jalapeno's had grown since its opening 14 years earlier. She wasn't surprised since the food and drinks of the local Mexican restaurant far outweighed many others in the local area. She was surprised to learn the history of the restaurant one day while sitting and talking with the owner at the Abercorn Street location. Arnold told her.

"Jalapeno's began as a wedding gift when I married *the boss's* Daughter Magda. I worked hard at Sombrero and truly loved the restaurant business. My wife has always been supportive. When we opened the first one here on Abercorn, Magda used to stand on the sidewalk waving a sombrero at the cars passing by. I love her and now we have seven different locations."

However, since opening a location in Pooler, Marie found she liked going to that location even more. The traffic was not as bad as Abercorn in Savannah. It's wasn't as close as the Abercorn location, but going there she was not interrupted by people who knew and recognized her as Hilton's wife.

Walking into the always busy restaurant, she noticed all the booths were taken. After being greeted by the hostess she smiled, saying, "I'll just take a seat at the bar, thank you."

Walking up to the bar she spotted a seat near a woman reading a book by one of the authors she picked up earlier.

"Excuse me, is someone sitting here?" Marie asked.

"No one is sitting here, go ahead." The woman said, flashing a pretty smile.

"How's that book, your reading?"

"It's actually really great. I have fallen for Treasure Blue and he's a great author."

"I just purchased one of his books from Barnes and Noble"

"Oh, I didn't know they were in B&N, I've gotten so hooked on this Kindle I haven't been there in a while."

"Do you enjoy reading books that way?"

"Excuse me ladies, what would you like to drink?" The bartender asked, interrupting their conversation.

"Monster Margarita's Raspberry Frozen," they said, in unison.

The two ladies fell out laughing, as they realized they ordered the same drink like they were old friends. Sitting there looking at each other smiling like school girls, Ms. Riley made the first introduction.

"Hi, I'm Nicole D. Riley; it's nice to meet you."

"Likewise, I'm Marie Chantel Scott. All my friends call me ReRe or Red."

Miss Riley smiled and said, "My sister name is Marie. You can call me Nikki almost everyone does."

Sitting and having a lively conversation like girlfriends Nikki realized how much she missed her old girlfriends and sister-n-laws. After her divorce, three years earlier she no longer had girlfriends to go kick it with as she was doing now with a complete stranger. She truly missed these times she silently thought as ReRe and she discussed the books, their lives and work.

Marie suddenly felt a connection to Nikki that she had never felt before. She was enjoying her mid-day lunch and the company. They discussed the books they were reading along with their lives and work. Nikki shared that since her divorce she had not been able to form a connection with another female friend. She owned a small brokerage company she ran from home. This didn't allow her the growth to connect with other women in the workplace.

She also shared her desire to have children. Marie told her about her kids JJ and Aryssa. Marie said they were her pride and joy. Aryssa was a little Princess and JJ thought he was, although being only five years old, the King Supreme. Marie and Nikki continued to talk for two hours sharing stories and book recommendations like old friends. Before they knew it, it was almost four o'clock. Looking at her watch, Marie jumped at the time. Seeing it had gotten so late. It had almost seemed like she had just arrived at the restaurant. She knew it was time to leave and pick up the kids from their afterschool programs.

"Nikki," Marie said, "Girl I really enjoyed meeting and hanging out with you, we definitely need to get together soon. How about, we meet back here tomorrow night for happy hour?"

"Really, that would be wonderful! I'm so happy you sat down beside me. We can definitely do that, here's my number and email address. I'm going to send you the link to my website."

Nikki handed Marie her business card and the two ladies hugged in a loving embrace like old friends. Marie handed Nikki her card also and hurried out of the restaurant.

Climbing into her car, Marie realized she was shaking. She had never felt such intense yearning before. While talking to Nikki their hands happened to brush each other and Marie could've sworn she felt electric currents passing through her body. She dismissed the notion quickly and continued to talk. However, during their departing embrace Marie could feel herself getting creamy and wet. She hoped she didn't show it when pulling out of the hug so quickly. She was in shock, sitting in the car, she could feel Nikki's breast as they touched her.

She wondered if they were as pretty as they were soft. Being a woman not as endowed as Nikki she silently thought how it would feel to touch and squeeze those breast between her teeth as she suckled them like a baby.

Coming out of her daydream, Marie shook her head effortlessly trying to figure where these desires and images were coming from. She had never been attracted to another woman before. She admired beautiful black women, but never had she entertained the thought of kissing and making love to one. Making a mental note to call her therapist later, Marie put the car in gear and headed to meet the kids.

Picking up the kids, they started sharing conversation about how school went and how their day was during the ride home. Marie laughed at how animated JJ had become while talking about a girl in his kindergarten class. Aryssa, on the other hand stated she wanted to spend the weekend at her best friend's house. And since the two girls shared the same birthday, Marie granted her request.

Upon arriving home, the kids headed to their rooms downstairs as Marie headed to her office. She had already received the email from Nikki, but didn't open it until she got home. Pulling up her computer, her heart pounded at the thought of sharing books and reading list with Nikki. Marie felt herself getting wet again, at the thought of sharing more with Nikki. As Marie smiled and shook her head again, she dismissed the notion. Maybe it was just the fact that she and Hilton had not had sex in five years which He always reminded her. Marie quickly pulled her thoughts back to the words on screen and read Nikki's email.

"Hi, Marie, I really enjoyed meeting you today. It seems we have lots in common. I can't wait till tomorrow it's been a long time since, I had a girlfriend to hang out with." Nikki

"Oh P.S. don't forget to order your Kindle Fire tonight. I just checked and they are on sale at Amazon.com. See ya soon." Nikki.

Marie was overwhelmed with emotions and excitement, all at the same time. She had never felt a connection so strong with anyone aside from Hilton. Hilton wasn't the only man she ever slept with, but he was the only man who excited her to the point of hearing his voice made her wet. As she sat there just staring at the computer screen lost in thought and trying to gain her composure, Marie knew it was time to reconnect with Hilton. Looking at her watch she knew he usually came in around 8 pm every week night. His businesses kept him busy and paid for everything they had. She was so proud of him. He never let anything keep him from going after his dreams. She wished she had his strength and determination. Marie wasn't naïve; she knew women threw themselves at Hilton left and right. Who could deny a man as handsome as he was? At that thought she knew only one could resist Hilton's charms, her.

He was a six foot two chocolate Adonis. His branches of Health and Fitness Gyms kept his body ripped and precisely cut in all the right places. When they first courted, Marie would always visit his gym on the Eastside of Savannah. After their engagement, she stopped going to his gyms. It wasn't that she did not support him; it was just hard seeing all the envious looks of the women that made her skin crawl. When she expressed the fact to Hilton that she was no longer comfortable in his facilities, Hilton being the man he was, partnered silently with another local gym and gave it to Marie as their second anniversary gift.

Marie suddenly became overwhelmed with guilt as she genuinely thought about how relentless Hilton had tried to get her to make love to him. He didn't press overbearingly but he was persistent nonetheless. Thinking about the events that had transpired earlier had her wet and creamy inside her silk panties. At that thought, Marie decided tonight would be the night. Tonight she would show Hilton that she was still in love with him and only him. She would prove to herself and to him that he was the only one she desired. Convincing herself to sleep with Hilton wasn't hard; she still thought he was the sexiest man she'd ever seen. In her heart Hilton was the only one for her. But inside her head at that very moment, Nikki was the one she desired.

Forcing herself up from the computer, Marie made her way to the shower to prepare for a night of love making with Hilton. Tonight she planned to wear some of the extra sexy lingerie he brought her from Adam and Eve. Strolling through her closet she found the perfect piece of lingerie that would definitely turn Hilton on. The sexy black leather cat suit mingled with fishnet across the breast and a pair of black Jimmy Choo knee high boots would send

Hilton's dick to attention as soon as he saw her. She remembered his excitement as she opened the present when the FedEx courier delivered it to her about four months ago. Yes tonight would definitely be a night for Hilton to remember. Marie, smiled as she hoped she would remember it to.

DESIRE'

After her chance meeting with Marie, Desire' felt a bit rejuvenated. She had not connected with another female in a long time and Marie offered a glimmer of hope. In her line of work the only other people she came into regular contact with were men. Even with all the mass changes in history men still dominated the transportation industry. Desire 'felt herself lucky to break into the industry back in the late nineties. Now she had transitioned from being behind the wheel to owning her very own company. A dream she thought would never come true after her marriage to Calvin Sellers. Calvin was a good looking man and he knew it. He didn't waste time sharing it with every woman he met either. Thinking back, Desire' wondered why she ever married such a man. One thing she had learned though was a cheetah could never change his spots.

Thinking back to when she first met Calvin at the Love's Truck stop while having a tire replaced, she wished she could go back to that day and slap the taste out his mouth. She'd never forget the day Calvin came up to her acting all macho. Being in a male dominated industry, Desire' was not a stranger to the way men reacted to seeing her anymore. And, normally, she ignored the comments and suggestive innuendos she received. But it was something about the swagger and confidence that Calvin wore like a second skin. It didn't hurt that those pretty brown eyes and white teeth accented a very handsome smile. At that time he wore a beard shaped into a thin line around his square jaw line. His bald head shimmered in the sunlight almost reflecting a glare. Calvin stood about seven inches taller than Desire' at her five foot frame. He had a fit body yet not as muscle bound and toned as Hilton. Yet he wasn't as many other truck drivers where you see their stomach before you see them. His voice was as commanding as his presence. When he spoke it was with authority, but not overtly controlling.

Desire' dated Calvin for two full years before accepting the marriage proposal that came three months into the relationship. She thought she had finally found love. She felt that finally at thirty years old, her heart's desire would finally come true. To have a family of her own! Desire' enjoyed life with Calvin while dating; they seemed to share many of the same wants and dreams. As a couple they were inseparable. Whenever they weren't working they were no more than five feet apart. Calvin used to joke that he could not stand to be farther away from her than her height. Desire' always found that amusing.

Calvin kept her smiling and laughing as they talked and shared dreams of a family and business they would own. Desire' first told Calvin of her dreams of owning a freight brokerage firm after they had been dating six months. Calvin promised her then that he would do whatever he could to make her dreams happen. Desire' at that moment decided the first dream she wanted was to become a mother. Being a child of adoption, Desire loved her family. All of them which included six sisters and brothers through her adopted mother. Then there was her biological family. She adored them, aside from her there were two brothers and a sister. They all shared the same mother but her oldest sister and younger brother had different fathers. During her childhood, Desire' always felt out of place. There were times where she didn't know where she belonged. When she reached her mid-teens that's when her mother came into play. Up until her 10th birthday, Desire' had no idea she was adopted, this happened to coincide with the worst year of her young life; the year she lost her Big Mama. Desire' felt as if the gods in heaven were playing a cruel joke on her. Big Mama was always there to protect her and keep her safe. Losing her was like losing a part of her very own soul. That was the year she met her biological mother Dena for the first time. Dena seemed to appear out of thin air after Big Mama's funeral. Standing there staring at Desire' like a Cheshire cat. Desire' was drawn to the woman who favored her but scared at the same time. Feeling uneasy Desire' clung to her older sister Jackie's hand with a deathly grip. When Jackie, felt her hands trembling she looked over out of her conversation to see what was wrong. Jackie nudged Lorraine and Richard to inform them that Dena had arrived. Shortly after Desire' was sent to another room while the adults talked things over. Life for Desire' was never the same after that. During the next seven years of her life Desire' virtually lived out of a suitcase. She hadn't spent more than a year in one steady home. From living with her oldest sister Lorraine who fell prey to the crack epidemic.

To going Richard, her brothers home, to Dena and Elton's house, to Ira, then Jackie's, then back to Dena's and finally landing in Jacksonville with her aunt and uncle at sixteen. Desire' had finally had enough.

Upon her seventeenth birthday Desire' had her bags packed and ready to go. This time she would not be going to another family member who didn't really want her she was going out on her own. And since then she remained on her own. Never looking back Desire' boarded a plane at Jacksonville International Airport headed for Gary Indiana, just south of Chicago where she would then catch a bus en-route to Morganfield, Kentucky. Desire' had caught a presentation at school during career day at her newest school Jean Ribault High, where they were talking about a national career program called Job Corps. The program was free. And the presenter captivated Desires' attention speaking of all the free opportunities being offered to at risk youth. Being two years behind her class, this was the perfect opportunity for Desire' to become someone and prove to herself and everyone else that she was somebody. Even if nobody wanted her! Desire' skipped school the very next day and signed up for the program. Because she had no legal guardian after rejecting Dena, she had no problem signing up as an adult. At that time the legal age for enrollment without parental permission was 17 years old.

Thinking back to happier times with Calvin, Desire' felt he offered her security, stability and the promises of a family with her own children that she could give her love. The first three years they shared together were some of her happiest times. The first year of their marriage Calvin gave Desire' everything he could think of. They built a home together, she went back to school and became a master broker and stopped driving a truck to stay at home and dispatch for Calvin's company. Life seemed to finally be giving Desire' some happy moments once again. Desire' knew she hadn't felt this much happiness since Big Mama died. Unfortunately for Desire' the saying began to ring true shortly after their first anniversary. A Cheetah can never change his spots. Just three short months after their first anniversary, Desire' started to notice changes in Calvin's behavior. No longer, did he want her to dispatch him and more and more he found ways to stay away from home overnight. Being a truck driver and a dispatcher Desire' knew what the road entailed. It wasn't like she was a stranger to this lifestyle but when you don't have to stay out why would you? The first time she confronted Calvin about his later than late nights, she was shocked by his response. That was the first time Calvin ever raised his voice and hands towards Desire', although never striking her, he grabbed her quickly, causing her to lose her balance and slightly stumble. At that very moment her image of him was shattered. Desire' knew there would be no turning back once violence came into play within a marriage and she refused to be one of those women who allowed men to beat them and still sleep in the same bed.

That very night after eating dinner and making love to Calvin as if nothing happened; Desire' waited until Calvin was in deep slumber. She knew the exact moment his sleep was getting good because he would always snore loudly and leave her warm embrace. He'd always end up on the other side of the bed. Desire' lay patiently waiting on the precise moment to arrive. Once she knew Calvin was sleeping peacefully, she got out of bed and headed to the guest room and retrieved her hope chest. Desire' hadn't opened the hope chest, which she really referred to as the FAN chest, since her and Calvin moved in together. Calvin had a severe dislike of the "Fuck a Nigga" chest and let her know to never to keep it in the house. Because Calvin had started spending so much time she thought it prudent to she moved the chest into the guest room from her storage unit.

Desire' opened her FAN chest quickly and removed the two pieces she had custom made. She owned a Ruger LC9 9MM Dao custom made in all purple, this was her favorite steel, not only because of its custom grape purple color but it packed a power punch. Shooting this gun at the range always drew the attention of many. Her other piece was a pretty shade of pink used by Hello Kitty. Kitty was also a Ruger but a smaller version.380. It was compact enough for Desire' to carry in her purse or on her without being intrusive. Desire' was afraid of guns until she met Vincent who took her to the woods in northern Kentucky and showed her the power of a handgun. Ever since that time, Desire' held her own pieces and was licensed to carry in three states. But for tonight, she thought Kitty would be enough to do the job. Removing Kitty from her double locked case, Desire' quietly walked back into her bedroom with where

Calvin still lay snoring in bed. Walking around to his side, Desire' climbed in bed atop of Calvin and slowly kissed her way down his stomach. This was her signal to Calvin that she wanted to please him and devour his chocolate goodness, so doing this only awakened his manhood as he lay back smiling. However, tonight, Desire had other plans in mind; as she felt his manhood grow, while trailing kisses down she quietly removed the custom Don Horton Knife and placed it at Calvin's blood engorged penis.

Silently she whispered in his ear, "Don't move Honey, or tonight you'll lose your prized possession."

Slowly Calvin opened his eyes and looked directly into Ms. Kitty. As Desire' sat on his chest she began to speak slow and precise.

"My love, I never thought it would come to this moment especially this soon. I am not the kind of woman you can put your hands on. I told you this! I was not joking. Even though you did not physically hit me, your intentions seemed to be leading that way. You know I will not tolerate that. I love you but with all I have been through in life I love me even more. This is the only reason you get a onetime pass. I have noticed your changes in behavior prior to today and if you ever think about raising your hands at me again. I won't hesitate to pull the trigger. Do you understand me?"

Nodding his head, Calvin signaled his understanding of what Desire had just said. At that she asked him if he would like for her to continue her pleasure moment. Unable to speak, Calvin just nodded. Desire removed her custom Don Horton Knife from Calvin's still hard penis and replaced it with her mouth. Keeping Ms. Kitty firmly in place, she with one hand pleased Calvin until he begged and pleaded with her to stop after spilling his seed in her mouth. Satisfied that her point had been proven she spit Calvin's seed on his chest and left him in bed as she retreated to the guest room for the night.

Waking up the next morning to an empty house Desire' knew her marriage was over. She walked into her bedroom to find only a note and rose left from Calvin.

"Honey, my Desire', I am so sorry that I grabbed you yesterday. I know what you said about your past. I briefly lost control. I love you and I will never hurt you in that way ever again. I'm headed to New York for an eleven am delivery, I will return home in two days. When I arrive I hope your still here and those damn guns are gone." Love Cal

Smiling to herself, Desire' smelled her rose and took the note to place inside her FAN chest, inside the wall in the guest room.

Honey's Kiss

Open them legs boo, it's the reversal show,

This time you're gonna be my ho,

My tongue I'll stick around the tip,

Gripping you firm around your hips,

Back to the bed, I got you floating on air

You're holding on tight, gripping my hair,

You buck and moan every time I go around,

I'm taking it slow going up and down,

The caress from my lips, and your arousal grow

Soft little hum, makes your sweetness flow

You scream my name through moans and sighs,

You love the way I work between your thighs,

I got your body jerking without a doubt,

When you scream, its Honey's name you shout

You scream and moan, I'm driving you insane

And tears flow free the moment you came

You crave our reversal show

'Cause Honey's kiss is always nice and slow

HILTON

Hilton was in no rush to get home. It seemed as though He couldn't get the night with Desire' out of his mind. Closing the documents on his desk as he was unable to complete the last few sentences he kept repeating over and over, Hilton felt a shiver of defeat welling up inside his brain. Imagines of Desire' kept popping up in his mind all day and it only seemed to get worse every time he looked at the framed photo of him and his wife sitting on his desk.

Snapping out of his daze, he decided to leave work and head over to Desires' house and have a light dinner. Heading out of the gym, he sent Desire' a message to make sure she was available. He hated disturbing her while she worked. Having a home business, he knew she was always home, yet she was no slacker. Desire' worked relentlessly at her craft which was one of the many things that had amazed him about her.

"Desire' my sweet; I wanted to see if you would like to have lunch. I can have it delivered in about forty-five minute, H."

Waiting on her reply, he pulled up the menu for Outback online and the numbers of the delivery service he often used to have meals sent to the workaholic she was. Desire' confessed once that she often went many days without realizing she hadn't eaten. Only with the smoking, that was one of the habits she wished she could break. Feeling the slight buzz from his cell, Hilton looked at the screen to see Desire' had quickly replied to his message.

"Hill, Sorry but I have just arrived back home from getting bite at Jalapeno's. I know I never get out but today was so slow that I decided to take your advice and get out and eat more. I'm so glad I did. I met a wonderful woman today and we hit it off really great. I'm meeting her tomorrow for happy hour, but after that we can get together. I'll be up working late tonight, D."

Feeling slightly disappointed Hilton, smiled anyway. Desire' truly was a wonderful woman who just needed to come out of her protective shell a bit more. He felt a small sense of pride that she had finally taken his advice. He knew she really missed hanging with the friends she had during her marriage, but couldn't understand why she didn't just call her girlfriends. Feeling that there really was more to the story, he never pressed her for information. He knew that in her own time she would tell him about their separation.

Still wanting some company before heading home, Hilton decided to call his good friend Chase to see if they could grab a bite. Chase had been his boy for a long time. He was thoroughly happy when Chase went into business for himself. Chase used to manage Hilton's west-side gym. That is until he decided to open up an all ladies facility for himself. Hilton was so proud of him that he backed him in opening a second location and giving it to his wife as a present. Although he didn't get involved in the operations, he stayed abreast of the financials and also knew every time his wife was there thanks to Chase. Chase worked hard to maintain both the facilities and contemplating opening a third location down in Richmond Hill. Chase worked just as hard as Hilton, which led them to not getting together as often as they liked. Nodding to himself, Hilton decided to call Chase so they could meet at the spot. Listening to Chase's call tune, he found himself bouncing to Rick Ross's, *The Boss*.

"I'm the biggest boss you've thus far."

"Beach bodies, Chase speaking."

"Maaaan, why did you answer so quickly? I was just getting into that Boss."

"Jake, man you know how I do. I'm trying to be like you when I grow up!"

"Man, save that, you already the Boss! I saw those financials you sent me this morning. Beach Bodies is doing quite well and that's what's up right there."

"I know right, I'm working so hard I hardly have time for anything else." "The construction down in Richmond Hill is moving along so quick I can barely keep up."

"Yeah that's why I am calling, how about tearing yourself away from the gym and give your managers a break."

"You must be reading my mind; I was just telling Black that I was starving."

"Cool, and then see you in Japan, forty-five minutes."

Hilton was beaming; he couldn't believe how far Chase had come in the last couple of years. He wasn't even affecting his business as Beach Bodies continued to grow. Hilton was very proud of him. Arriving at Season of Japan, Hilton ordered hot sake and sat near the back while waiting on him to arrive.

Sitting he thought back to Desire', glad that she was making new friends and getting out just a little bit more. Although he was happy for her, he silently wished she was available for him tonight. Deep in thought while taking bites out of his Spider Roll, savoring the soft shell crab, he hadn't noticed Chase walking into the restaurant.

"Man, you must be a million miles away." Chase stated, while taking a seat in the booth. Snapping out of his daze Hilton gave his boy a pound, while swallowing the last of the food in his mouth.

Over the next hour and half, Hilton and Chase talked about everything from the NBA play-offs tithe construction of his new building in Richmond Hill. They both enjoyed the banter and realized they needed to get together even more often. The sushi was good and filling and they ordered another round of the delicious rolls that included Samurai, Spider, Rainbow and Red Dragon rolls. Finishing off the sake and ordering more, Chase brought up the subject he knew Hilton was avoiding.

"Man, I haven't seen Marie in the gym in a couple of days, have things gotten better between you too yet?"

"Things between us are just as they have been the last five years. Our anniversary was last week and I went all out all week long. I sent her everything I could think of and she still didn't give me any." Shaking his head Hilton sighed, continuing. "You know I love my wife, but to be honest man, I don't see her, the same anymore. I'm not in love with her anymore. I mean, I'm not leaving her. I can't do that to my children. We just exist; we are more like roommates than husband and wife. I just don't know what to do or how to do it."

Chase sat silently listening to his mentor describe all the things he had done to prove to his wife she meant more to him than anything. After a few minutes Chase knew he had to say something. He just didn't understand why Hilton continued to be faithful to a woman who rejected him for so long.

"I know you don't want to hear this Hilton, but I told you before you need to get some. There are discreet ways to relieve the pressure and tension. I don't know how you have survived this long. I know that lotion and baby oil is taking a toll, Palmetta needs a break man."

Laughing at the advice from Chase, Hilton decided to tell him about Desire'. He had never spoken about her to anyone and the images of the night before played in his head. Hilton decided to share the night's event with Chase. Knowing the conversation wouldn't go any further than the two of them Hilton broke the news to Chase about Desire'.

"Well speaking of being discreet, I heard what you've been saying," Hilton remarked.

Chase stopped chewing quickly replacing it with a smile as he stared at Hill. "Man, please tell me, you've met someone and got some please. I was about to put you in a monastery."

Laughing Hilton replied, "Slow down dude, I did meet someone and we've been building a friendship for a couple years now. And up until the other night that's all it was. I can't seem to get her out my mind now. I just don't know, man. She is a wonderful woman, sweeter than a Georgia peach." Hilton said, while licking his lips.

Chase had his mouth open so wide flies could go in and out unnoticed as he listened to Hilton talk about Desire', his mystery woman. Frowning slightly, Chase broke into the conversation and wanted to know why he was just now finding out about Desire'. "How you gonna act, you been kicking it with another woman for a couple years and I am just now hearing about it? Man I thought we were cool." Chase laughed out loud.

Hilton couldn't help but laugh as Chase sat there looking like his son did when he pouted. Hilton felt relief at finally telling someone about Desire'. He was amazed at how animated he got while talking about Desire', she made him smile unknowingly. Hilton somehow felt that Chase would see him in a different light now that he had confessed his feelings for Desire' and voiced his opinion to Chase apologetically.

"Hilton", Chase said, "You have nothing to apologize for seriously. I have been telling you for the last four years, that you needed to take matters into your own hands. You and Marie are like family to me, but as a man I can't see why you put up with that so long. Until you told me, I never knew you were having such a hard time in your marriage. No one would have guessed it, to see the two of you together. I know you love her, but as my mentor, let me tell you I would have been spanking somebody else's ass a long time ago. That's why I'll never get married!" Chase shrugged and replied. "Man don't feel bad, you are a rare breed of a man, because any other man would've been getting some on the side. Shit, I was about to put you up on the BackPages and pimp yo' ass out for real."

At the mention of BackPages the two men fell out laughing again. Hilton no longer felt as conflicted as he was. He was relieved to express some of his feelings to Chase. Being as private as he was, Hilton didn't openly discuss his marriage or private affairs with anyone other than Chase. And in all the years he had known him nothing that they discussed ever was revealed to anyone else. Chase was his boy one hundred percent. Hilton felt so much better as he paid the bill. Only allowing Chase to pay the tip, he left their favorite spot smiling as he headed home.

Walking into his house, Hilton thought he was dreaming. He expected to see JJ and Aryssa lounging in the den, but what he found was Marie standing in the doorway wearing nothing but a red body stocking. Mesmerized he stood looking at a vision of beauty. Marie was standing and posing in a pair of platform heels that matched the revealing undergarment, Hilton just stood there with his mouth open. He had not seen his wife looking like this in five years. This was one of the many garments he had bought from Adam & Eve trying to get her to make love to him. Now there she stood looking like a sexy devil, with a red butterfly thong peeking through the crotchless stocking accenting her breasts with a straight cut neckline, while boosting up her already erect nipples. Her short hair was pushed back by the little headband that had devilish little red horns on top. Hilton's dick quickly stood at attention looking at the woman he loved standing in the doorway appearing as if she had just posed for a magazine shoot advertising the garment. Snapping out of his gaze, Hilton found himself scooping up his wife while racing to the middle of the room.

Bracing herself for what was about to happen, Marie found herself hoping that this little session with her husband wouldn't take long as she lay back on the floor her mind drifted off to Nikki as she allowed her husband to make love to her for the first time in five years.

"I can't wait." he uttered, fumbling with the belt on his pants, he panted while successfully pulling his pants off.

Reaching up and kissing him hard, she fantasized that his lips were Nikki's. Marie couldn't believe that she couldn't get Nikki out of her mind.

"Fuck me," she began to whisper over and over in Hilton's ear. "Fuck me now!"

At her request, Hilton obliged. A small moan escaped his lips as his mouth covered her breast, surprise ripped through him as he slipped his fingers inside her already wet vagina while searching for the small bump of her G-spot. Moaning and breathlessly breathing her name, Marie was miles away as she replayed Nikki's smile over and over in her mind as her husband made love to her.

He drew tiny circles around her hardened nipples as his fingers worked overtime inside her becoming soaked as her wetness grew. The only words, she could muster out of her mouth without calling out for Nikki, was fuck me, as she pleaded for Hilton to take her. Switching positions and taking the lead, Marie knew the only way to hurry this up was for her to take command. Sitting up, Hilton smiled as she quickly mounted his engorged dick she began to move up and down on him, slowly at first but with increasing speed. He smiled looking up at her and admiring how beautiful she looked at that very moment. He groaned deeply with each squeeze crushing his manhood inside her. Engaging her pelvic floor and drawing her pussy tighter Marie knew in a matter of seconds Hilton would no longer be able to contain him.

At that thought she threw her head back in the air and the image of Nikki sitting at the bar appeared again. She moaned, grabbed Hilton's hands placing them from her waist to her breast. Moving strategically her grinding began to quicken, while continuously squeezing her pelvic muscles in pace with her bouncing ass. With each descent she could feel his pressure building, begging for release. She looked down at her husband's smiling face seeing the tears streaming out of his eyes while calling her name. She quickly increased the pace. Succumbing to her riding him hysterically, like she was in another world, Hilton felt his seed about to spill. Grabbing her waist, Marie felt his body seize as he sat up quickly pulling her into his embraced as his hot rapid ejaculation with her exploded. She stopped and held him close as her eyes closed images of Nikki appeared and once again she smiled.

Unable to believe what had just happened, Hilton sat there as his wife retreated to their bedroom without uttering so much as a single word other than fuck me, fuck me now. He was shocked. For the last five years all he wanted to do was make love to his wife. Over and over he pleaded and begged. Now as he lay there on the floor half-naked in shock, he couldn't believe that every time he closed his eyes all he saw was Desire'. Here he was engaged in sex with his wife and all he kept wishing was to open his eyes and see Desires' sweet peach inside his face. Hearing the shower, snapped him out of his gaze as he stood, shaking his head hoping the thoughts would leave his mind.

RED

Racking her brain, Marie tried to remember the last time she enjoyed sex with her husband. It had to be nearly six years ago being that JJ was now five going on fifty. After his birth she just didn't feel the same loving attraction to him. She knew that she didn't want a divorce or another man. She just could not see herself with anyone else. That is...

Stepping out of the shower, Marie knew for a fact Hilton would be sleeping. Even though it has been a long time since they were intimate, some things never changed. Standing in the doorway in a towel she confirmed her thoughts. Hilton was knocked out; he apparently showered in the guest bath. Lying flat on his back covering half the huge bed, Hilton lay sleeping with just a fresh pair of boxers on.

Instead of joining him in bed Marie, retreated to her office to check emails and take a look at Facebook before going to the gym. Scanning her emails she quickly sent all the junk into the trash bin. Seeing Nikki's email, made her smile. Although Marie had plenty of girlfriends there was something about Nikki that drew her to the woman in more ways than one. Remembering that she had ordered her Kindle Fire for overnight delivery, Marie leapt from the computer to retrieve the packages off the table that she brought in earlier that day. She had only ordered one Kindle Fire but there were three packages addressed to her. Without a doubt she knew the other two were from Hilton. Opening the first box she discovered an array of sex toys. Sitting the box aside slightly disgusted, she proceeded to the next one which smelled like one of her favorite treats. Smiling as she opened the box of Shari's Berries. Taking one of the berries out and placing in her mouth while grabbing the other box that contained her Kindle Marie made a mental note to send Nikki a box of the berries tomorrow after they met for happy hour.

Looking at the new Kindle in her hand, Marie smiled as she grabbed another berry and strolled back to the computer to email Nikki that it had arrived. Placing the kindle on her desk Marie found Nikki's email and sent her a reply.

"Hi, Nikki; I got my Kindle today, I had it delivered overnight. I am going to set it up right now so that I can get into the digital age with you, lol. I had a great time the other day can't wait till tomorrow for happy hour." See ya soon, ReRe."

Smiling and humming to herself, Marie then hurried over to Amazon.com to set her account up and order the books Nikki had suggested. Following her suggestions and liking all the authors' pages that she purchased. Marie was amazed at the number of unknown African American writers that were publishing books. She made mental notes to make sure she purchased several more books.

Distracted by the dinging of her email, she looked over to see that Nikki had reply quickly to her message. Opening the email she saw the small note that indicated that Nikki also was geeked about getting together for happy hour. She didn't have time to chat but left her Skype name and said she'll be available early tomorrow since she was working late to be free for tomorrow night. Satisfied that she was building a new friendship, Marie decided instead of working out in the home gym that Hilton had built for her, she would go to Beach Bodies and get in a solid workout, instead. Marie loved going to Beach Bodies it was one gift from Hilton that she treasured most. Chase, the co-owner and Hilton's friend had always been her trainer. She thoroughly enjoyed the way he pushed her to the limits in working out. They worked together in a great combination. Beach Bodies, unlike HardCores was an all-female gym. They offered diverse classes aimed at different body types and fitness levels to appeal to a wide variety of women. Marie was thrilled when Chase informed her that the gym was now a 24 hour facility.

Other new amenities were full time security and a car service so the women would feel safe at any hour coming to the gym. Another new feature was the girl fight nights. Several members had expressed gratitude for the new kick boxing and self-defense classes as well...changing into a coral splice block tee and matching shorts, Marie grabbed a jacket and pants of the same set and headed out the door. Realizing another thing that she and Nikki may be able to do together she made a mental note to bring it up tomorrow at happy hour.

Before heading out she left Hilton a note indicating where she was headed. Although she didn't feel the need to keep tabs on his whereabouts at all times she always let him know where she was.. It took little effort to be courteous, and being his wife, she felt it was her job to always let him know where she would be especially when leaving the house after midnight. It was just something she did.

Heading to the gym there were only two things on her mind, Nikki and a good workout. Coincidentally, those things although totally different, could lead to the same thing. Her with a, hot and sweaty body.

The strongest thoughts however were of being touched by Nikki. Trying to get control of her emotions and the hormones that were raging inside her body that was causing a river between her legs, Marie turned the radio on to E93 instead of her satellite. She listened to the local station in the mornings in order to catch the Strawberry Letter. Thinking about that maybe she should write to Shirley Strawberry and Steve Harvey, she thought maybe, just maybe they could shed some light on her newest dilemma. She just couldn't seem to get Nikki out of her head. It was more than just a new friendship that captured her, but the feelings she let loose unknowingly. Marie had never felt attracted to women until then. It was so strange and exciting at the same time. She always thought women were the greatest gift God created for the human eye. Yet, it was always just admiring the form. Women have bodies of Goddess and many don't even realize it. Marie didn't just admire sexy sleek slim women; some of the women she admired were full-figured plush women. Pretty faces, big smiles and natural beauties had always captured Marie's attention. Although she always admired women, being with a woman had never crossed her mind. It definitely had never had her daydreaming about them. She would definitely write that letter to the morning show and see what they thought.

Arriving at the gym, she noticed Chase's burgundy Caddy. Laughing she could see why he couldn't keep a girlfriend. Aside from being a workaholic, that man had a serious addiction to restoring cars. Marie often teased the trainer about being a candy paint addict, as she jumped out the car and headed inside the gym.

Pulling out all the stops, Marie worked out extremely hard. She was coming off the treadmill when she spotted Chase talking to one of the night attendees. Walking over to say Hi, she stopped dead in her tracks and headed in another direction after seeing the woman he was talking too. Throwing the towel over her head and heading to the bathroom, she was visibly shaking. It could not be her, not here, not now Marie stopped. Pulling out her cell she decided to text Nikki and make sure.

"Hey Nikki, I was just taking a break from my workout at the gym and decided to see what you were up too. I know you said you'd be up late hope, I didn't wake you, ReRe."

Waiting for a reply, Marie paced back and forth in the stall hoping the images in her head were playing tricks on her mind and that was not Nikki, Chase was hitting on. Calming down, Marie thought she was seeing RED and decided to put some cool water on her face. Standing in front of the mirror she realized she really needed to get herself together. This thing she had for Nikki was getting the best of her. She thought as her cell phone vibrated with a message from Nikki.

"ReRe, no you didn't wake me, I was just closing out another transaction here for two more shipments going to New York tomorrow and Thursday. Why are you at a gym this late? Is it safe? I've been thinking of joining one. You should fill me in tomorrow at happy hour. TTYL! Nik"

Breathing a sigh of relief, Marie splashed more water on her face in hopes of shaking off the feelings she was having. It was unrealistic for her to be reacting in such a way. She had never even felt jealous for seeing women come at Hilton. Now here she was standing in the bathroom seeing RED all because she mistook another woman for Nikki. Marie felt like she must be having a nervous breakdown. She was too young for a mid-life crisis still shy of forty by two years. She needed to return to seeing her therapist. She resigned to the fact that something must be wrong with her. Going back to see her therapist was a must. Splashing more water on her face she grabbed her towel opting not to shower at the gym and head towards her car. She'd have to talk with Chase another time.

Driving home, Marie turned to her favorite Jazz station; she needed something to calm her down. It was one thing to be fantasizing about Nikki but on another different level to actually want to do bodily harm to her friend because she thought he was talking to her. Chase was a good man, but he had women all over him all the time. His mixed heritage was to blame. Being biracial Chase had the prettiest eyes she'd ever seen on a man. The long lashes complemented his beautiful green eyes. It was those eyes that had Chase with more women than he could handle, but there was no way she would let him have her Nikki.

MARIE

After leaving the gym, Marie was fit to be tied. She was still seeing Red. Her jazz station wasn't helping to soothe her. Touching the screen on her radio, she quickly found IHeart Radio; the song playing came blaring through her speakers sending her into a better mood instantly as she sang along with El, Al, Barry White and others.

"I wanna read your mind, know you deepest feelings I wanna make it right for you..."

But when Barry White started talking her mind went berserk. With thoughts of Nikki, then to top it off *Lady in My Life* by Michael Jackson played next. The song took on a whole new meaning for Marie as she listened to Michael's voice crooning in her ears. She did not know which was worse, feeling sad over his sudden death or the feelings another woman elicited in her head.

As she rounded the corner before getting home, Whitney Houston began to sing her infamous song *I Will Always Love You* This song brought her to a time she hadn't visited in many years. Hilton had a beautiful young girl serenade her with this song before JJ was born. It was a morning during which she had been confined to bed because of Pre-eclampsia. At the beginning of her last trimester, her doctor insisted on strict bed rest. She had gained a lot of weight with JJ and during that time felt purely un-pretty. She didn't want to tell Hilton how she felt about having JJ for fear he may resent her but one morning after pressing her to talk to him about something insignificant. She carelessly blurted out it was his entire fault that she was a hideous and ugly fat woman. Stating she hoped the child she carried beneath her heart would love her because she wasn't feeling love from him. Hilton held his head down leaving the room. When he returned with a full staff to take care of everything from her head to toe, all she could do was cry. She was full of emotions. Hilton knew the hormones made her say the things she had.. He apologized for making her feel less than the beautiful woman she was.

"No matter how much weight, how your hair looks what your clothes look like or anything else I will always love you Marie."

At that very moment a beautiful girl stepped from behind Hilton singing Whitney's version of the song, which stunned Marie. She would have never believed that the CD was not playing had she not witnessed the young lady belting her heart out. It was so beautiful. She cried and apologized for her behavior.

The housekeeper stayed on staff full-time until after JJ's first birthday. Remembering that moment, calmed Marie down, as she pulled in her driveway. She decided not to park in the garage, because she left her garage door opener and didn't want to wake Hilton. Entering the code on the front door, Marie walked into her home. They rarely used the door since they mainly parked in the garage. It was close to three a.m. and Marie wasn't the least bit sleepy. Heading to the shower she decided to lounge in the den and sip on a little chamomile tea while reading a book. That, she figured would be enough to put her in a sleepy mood.

Steeping her favorite tea, Marie savored the smell of the rich floral fragrances and fresh cut apple blossoms, emitting from her tea cup. Chamomile was her favorite tea, and adding just a little honey, enhanced the sweetness. She made a slice of whole grain wheat toast with peanut butter and a banana to go with her tea. The combination of peanut butter, banana and tea would definitely put her to sleep.

Taking her new Kindle and snacks she headed for the den. She wanted to get some reading in before happy hour tomorrow, so she and Nikki could converse more over the books. Smiling to herself, she knew books weren't the only thing she wanted to talk over with Nikki.

HAPPY HOUR

Desire' decided to pass the time away
by beginning a new entry in her journal.

How can I feel the warmth of your
body as I think about you night after lonely
night? The sweetness of your kisses from
lips I have never felt? Why does my body fill
up with butterflies as I wait patiently to hear
your voice or see your smile? How can the
images of you fill my mind moment after
moment? Why are these feelings arising
within me so suddenly? Am I losing my
mind and going insane? I feel as if I'm riding
a rollercoaster of emotions. Do you feel the
same electric currents pulsing through your
body as I do?

Am I a hypocrite, yes or no? Maybe I
am. I finally see how easy it is for a man or
woman to cheat on the person they love. But
is it real love or lust that I am feeling? How

can he love her so much but desire me? Can you truly love someone you can never have? With such a passion that your heart skips a beat at the mere thought of them. When I close my eyes at this very moment will I see your face or another?

Leaving the journal entries Desire' decided to check her emails, quickly deleting all the junk mail. Finding a couple of new load entries in her outlook mailbox Desire found herself posting a couple of bids for freight moving from New York to Miami. Checking to see how many units she had in the area, Desire sent the bids through; since it was still early she had time to negotiate some more bids before getting ready for Happy Hour with ReRe.

Thinking of ReRe, made her smile. At first she thought it was just the idea of having a new girlfriend to kick it with. But thinking back over the evening she suddenly felt a little more may be in store for her. She thought how overly attentive ReRe was to everything she said. Then when she hugged her before leaving, Desire could've sworn that she could hear ReRe exhale during their brief embrace. Then as she exchanged cards she noticed her slightly trembling. Shaking her head, admonishing herself, she remembered ReRe, talking about her children and husband. Desire' knew her overactive imagination was taking hold of her. Dismissing the notions Desire' decided to start to prepare for Happy Hour and just enjoying having a new girlfriend.

MARIE

Waking up to soft kisses all over her face, Marie smiled as images of Nikki played behind her eyelids. Not wanting the pleasure to stop she reached out to caress the face of the woman who brought back desire into her life. Reaching out, she felt the face of her husband and sat up with a jolt. Slightly disoriented, Marie stared at Hilton wondering what was going on. Hilton seeing the state his wife was in decided to torment her just a bit.

"Well, why is my lovely wife sleeping in the den moaning so loud and waking me out of my sleep?"

"Stop playing Hill, as loud as you snore, a freight train couldn't wake you. And you're completely dressed so how could I wake you."

"Well, I haven't heard you moaning in your sleep in ages, you dreaming about me babe?"

"Of course."

"Stop lying ReRe, it probably was Idris again!"

"Well just for that I am not tell you, ha!"

Smiling at his beautiful wife, Hilton inquired about what Marie had planned for the day, and if she was available for lunch for the day? Finally rising out of the recliner, Marie told Hilton about going to Happy Hour with a friend and doing some more reading. Giving her a kiss, Hilton headed out to begin his usual day at the office. Having four locations throughout Savannah was not an easy task. As he rose to leave, Hilton looked back at his wife and mouthed "I love you darling." Smiling, Marie winked and headed down to their bedroom to shower and prepare for the day.

Plopping down on their bed, Marie exhaled loudly and fell back into the plush comforter on the massive bed. Shaking her head side to side, she couldn't believe the realness of her dream. When Hilton began kissing her she was dreaming about Nikki at the bar after their first meeting. She was replaying flashes in her head as the kisses rained down on her reality. Glad that she wasn't a sleep talker, she could only giggle at the look on Hilton's face as he stared at her telling her she was moaning again.

Knowing it had truly been a long time since she had dreams of that nature, the moaning in her sleep did not occur often. She knew Hilton probably felt it was because of their love making session last night and truthfully she knew Nikki was to thank for that. Stretching out along the bed Marie came across an envelope tucked in between the pillows. Opening the card Marie read the sweet sentiment Hilton had left for her. Tossing the card back on the bed, Marie turned the IHeart radio on and began to sing along while heading to the shower.

Arriving at Jalapeno's a bit early was a good idea, Marie thought as she parked alongside the curbside close to the grass. The atmosphere was intoxicating as were the drinks. Barely getting inside the door, the fiesta music was blaring loudly as Sombreros' flew in the air. There was someone having a birthday party and the wait staff clapped enthusiastically while singing the popular "Happy happy birthday, happy birthday to you!"

Standing next to the bar trying to place an order, Marie waited patiently on the bartender to take her order. When she finally got his attention she ordered a shot of Patron gold. She was quite nervous and needed something to take the edge off before Nikki arrived. Listening to the conversation going on beside her Marie, giggled slightly as the much older Caucasian man tried to pick up the young Latino waitress. It never ceased to amaze her at some of the pick-up lines people used to try and get numbers. The male was busy telling the young waitress that he could be her sugah daddy. Don't let the gray hair on top fool you, Marie heard him say as he left her a ten dollar tip.

Leaving the bar to wait outside for Nikki, Marie was feeling calmer. Looking down at her phone Marie replied to several text messages and sent one to Hilton. Feeling the slight effects of the Patron gold, she jiggled her head to the familiar sounds over the speakers coming from inside the restaurant. Smiling to herself, Marie knew they were in for a great time tonight.

As Marie noticed Nikki walking past the dry cleaners down the side walk, she felt the sudden rush of anxiety kick in as her yoni begins to twitch. Feeling the need to do something, Marie walked in Nikki's direction. However this proved to not be such a good idea, with the constant throbbing between her legs she felt her creaminess grow. Smiling at Nikki, she admired her walk. Even though she was larger than Marie's own petite frame, Nikki sashayed with confidence. Her ass demanded attention as she passed the men and women who were also waiting to enter the very busy restaurant. It was Thirsty Thursday in Jalapeno's and at that moment Marie was very thirsty.

Sitting at their booth Nikki and Marie both ordered Raspberry Monster Margarita's. While waiting on their drinks to arrive, the waitress brought over the normal chips and dip. The salsa was freshly made daily and was fiery. Seeing the salsa, Nikki quickly requested some of the queso to go with the salsa.

"You must be reading my mind; I was just about to ask for some dip." Marie stated.

Laughing, Nikki smiled and responded we have a lot in common.

Sitting in the booth close to the dance floor, the two women shared lively conversation on a variety of topics. The fiesta atmosphere continued to expand as the crowd engulfing the dance area grew. Bouncing to the array of music being played, the women were thoroughly having a good time. As the waitress approached their table again, Marie decided that along with another Margarita she would indulge in another quick shot. The waitress quickly asked if Nikki would like to have a shot also. Feeling the vibes in the room Nikki obliged. Not being much of a drinker she replied make that two; with a smile. Watching Nikki sway in her seat Marie was amazed at her vocal skills as Nikki sang along to a popular Adele tune. Switching the conversation to the musical selections being played Marie inquired what music Nikki liked.

Nikki was feeling ecstatic tonight. She was having a very good time; Marie was very entertaining as she continued to casually touch Nikki's hand. Nikki was about to ask her if she was enjoying the evening when the waitress appeared with their drinks and another round of chips and salsa. Looking at the shots Marie, quickly ordered another round before the waitress was too far out of earshot. Taking the shots in hand Marie offered a toast to new friendships. Tapping their glasses together; they threw the shots down and grabbed the lime wedges and took a long squeeze. Arriving with the second round of shots Nikki thanked the waitress, as they both bounced in their seats to the sounds of Daddy Yankee.

The dance floor was getting more and more crowded as people danced and gyrated to the popular musicana. It was turning into a bigger fiesta by the moment. Marie was smiling and shimming in her seat when she saw a man walking towards them from the dance as the musical selection was changing!

"Mami, you look bueno, would you like to dance?" he asked Nikki

Blushing, Nikki quickly replied, "Sure only if we can dance together, me and my girlfriend here?"

Smiling hugely, the Spanish gentleman could hardly contain his excitement as he replied, "Si Mami," extending one of his hand to Nikki and the other to Marie. Taking his hands in unison, the trio headed to the dance floor as an abrupt round of shouts erupted on the floor when the familiar sounds of Marc Anthony featuring Pit Bull.

"Ay ay ay, let it rain over me, ay ay ay...."
The music was lively as they danced and swayed with the Spanish gentlemen. He was moving between Nikki and Marie simultaneously, as the dipped and bumped and swayed to the music enjoying the beats.

As the song was ending, he placed his hands around their waists and headed to the bar. When suddenly he spun the two ladies around as *International Love* blared through the speakers, Marie and Nikki found themselves in the middle of the dance floor swinging and alternating positions in front of the man who was dancing and lip syncing the lyrics to Pit Bull.

Next, The Black-eyed Peas song *Boom Boom Boom* came on the floor erupted again and Marie and Nikki found themselves surrounded as they popped and bounced, dropping to the floor whenever the chorus came up. They were having a blast as they danced through the next two songs with their mystery man. Finally feeling out of breath and in need of a drink the three headed towards the bar again as a slower song replaced the much faster pop beats. Standing at the bar, the mystery man said his name was Ricardo and that he would pay for another round of shots and their drinks if they would give him one more dance.

Feeling pumped and excited the two women agreed as they excused themselves and headed to the restroom to freshen up.

Standing in line waiting for an empty stall, Marie and Nikki grabbed some paper towels to clear up the perspiration streaming down their faces. Glad that the neither of them wore much makeup they begin to giggle like school girls while reaching in their pockets at the same time to reapply their gloss. The sounds of Adele's *Someone like You* began to place over the speaker system and Nikki began to sing.

"I swear that girl is singing that song, but your voice is beautiful."

"Awe thanks Marie, it's nothing special. I sing a lot while I am working"

Facing her, Marie said, "You really have a beautiful voice you should do it more often."

Standing there chatting neither of them noticed that the restroom had been emptied and they were just standing there talking. The women turned to face the mirror again and Nikki applied more of her gloss as Marie stood just gazing at Nikki. Unable to control the urges beginning to surge within, Marie found herself moving behind Nikki in the mirror.

Looking around and not seeing anyone else in the room. Marie placed her hand on Nikki's shoulder and turned her around facing her. Marie moved some stray pieces of hair from Nikki's face as she smiled.

"Nikki you are very beautiful."

"Marie, girl you must be feeling a little bit high, because I'm cute but not beautiful."

Marie glanced away, looking towards the door. When she looked back at Nikki, she opened her mouth to speak and no words came out. Again she glanced at the doorway, and when she turned around she moved closer to Nikki. Inside the restroom alone the women were standing face to face. Marie being slightly taller than Nikki leaned in towards her ear and whispered.

"You're more than cute; you are very beautiful and full of desire." Inhaling her scent Marie pulled back and gazed in Nikki's eyes.

The women were intoxicated. Nikki smiled as Marie looked into her eyes and leaned in placing her lips on full on Nikki's mouth. Shocked at what she had done, Marie pulled back quickly. Not seeing any resistance from Nikki, Marie leaned in again and this time with more hunger in her lips, she kissed Nikki passionately. She took her emblazoned tongue and twirled it inside Nikki's mouth as her shaking hands found Marie's head. She took her bottom lip between her teeth as Marie reached out and stroked her wet breast. Their kiss was hot and passionate as the women pulled apart out of breath and slightly embarrassed as they heard the door swing open as a couple of women sauntered into the restroom. Without looking at each other again the women re-applied their gloss and headed back to their booth.

Making their way across the dance floor back to their seats, both women seemed lost in emotion equally hot and full of fire. They quickly ordered another shot from the passing waitress while requesting the bill.

Sitting across from each other, Marie spoke first. "I am sorry; I don't know what came over me."

Looking flush, and feeling her heart pounding in her chest, Nikki smile and told Marie she had never kissed a girl. Smiling as the waitress brought the last shots; Nikki looked in Marie's eyes and said four words that made Marie smile like a Cheshire cat.

"But I liked it!"

Tossing back their shots, the women grabbed the lime wedges and savored the stole moment from moments ago.

SEEING EYES

For every action, there is a reaction. For every rejection, there is hurt. For every hurt, there is vengeance.

Cole could not believe his eyes at the images before him. In a dimly lit spot near the bar, Cole drained the last of his beer. Looking up to order another round, in hopes of drowning his sorrows his eyes caught a glimpse of the one whom was driving him to drinking heavily. He was unable to believe that she continuously rejected his advances. For thirteen years he had tried unsuccessfully to gain her affections. As his eyes watched her every fluid movement, Cole recalled the night she confessed to no longer sleeping with her husband, as they chatted over a working dinner. He had to practically drag it out of her. As they went over the reports, Cole poured her several glasses of wine while making small talk about her home life and marriage. Sensing her reluctance, Cole reached over and gently stroked the nape of her neck, while empathetically assuring her she could tell him anything. Once he sensed her defenses lowering he switched his questions from her and the children to her and Hilton.

As the tears welled up in her eyes, Marie told him everything she had not been able to tell anyone including Hilton. Watching her at this very moment, he knew that she still wasn't sleeping with her husband. The six month leave of absence proved that she was unhappy in her current situation. How could she not see all the love he could give her? She was his perfect mate. Every effort he had put forth had been rejected and dismissed over and over again. He had grown tired and was on the brink of giving up the fight, yet now the times seem to have changed for him. Moving a little closer to the dance floor for his eyes confirmed what his heart already knew. It was her. Here she was popping and gyrating on the floor with another woman and man.

Blazing heat began to surge within him so quickly he almost cracked the glass he was holding on to tightly. As beads of sweat began to form on his forehead, Cole quickly grabbed his cell phone and began to snap picture after picture. With his eyes tightly focused on a vision of beauty, his mouth formed a smug grin as his lips turned upwards. One way or another he silently vowed that she would become his.

As the current selection was ending they headed off the dance floor towards where Cole was sitting. Thinking quickly Cole did not want to be noticed. Sliding in between two other patrons, Cole stood close enough to eavesdrop on the conversation the three were having. With his phone handy, Cole recorded the names of the two unknown people surrounding his beloved.

Tossing back the rest of his drink, Cole wondered if he should interrupt the conversation. Seeing her in this setting had him wondering why she never smiled at him so lovingly. Angling his head so she would not be able to see his face, he decided to admire her from afar. It was best until he was able to confirm the identity of the two unknowns.

As he watched the two of them saunter away towards the restroom, he decided to descend upon the other. Making his way over; he abruptly stopped as he took note of the man hitting on the waitress at the bar. Seeing him as no immediate threat, Cole took his picture along with the waitress, who giggled at what was being said to her.

Devising a plan to bring his love to him, he would have now included the two unknowns as well as the main threat. He would no longer be denied. She would be his, even if she didn't know it yet.

DESIRE'

Hailing a taxi, the women were fit to be tied. They laughed and giggled the entire ride to Marie's lakeside home. Touching the side of Nikki's face, Marie tried to convince her to stay in the guestroom.

"Trust my husband is more than likely sleeping at this moment and it would be no trouble for you to stay."

"Maybe next time, I have a lot of bills to work on in the morning."

Looking at the truck in the driveway, Desire' shook off the thought, it couldn't be. Feeling a little more than anxious to leave after seeing Hill's truck, Desire' gave Marie a quick hug and waited until she went inside before giving the driver her address. Sitting in the back, lost in thought she was slowly putting the information racking her brain together. Hill's loveless wife is ReRe. How could it be, she pondered. It seemed to her as there was something missing behind the story.

She had never fully questioned Hill concerning his wife, she only allowed him to divulge the information as he felt comfortable with. Meeting ReRe felt like a breath of fresh air, now Desire' felt like the air was being drawn out of her lungs. Pulling out her cellphone she looked at the pictures she had snapped of ReRe and herself after dancing with Ricardo. She felt like an old friend. Could it possibly be that this is Hill's wife? Sighing loudly she wondered what had she allowed herself to get into? Thinking this is some Jerry Springer type episode, "Woman has affair with husband and wife." She could see the marquee scrolling through her closed eyes as her thoughts drifted back to the kiss in Jalapeño's. Sitting in the back of the taxi, her senses were still on high alert when the car came to an abrupt stop. Coming out of her daze, Desire' opened her purse to give the driver another tip, since ReRe had already paid the fare. Pulling out a ten to hand to the driver, Nikki noticed how sinister his grin was. Quickly grabbing her keys she opened the door and handed the driver his tip.

Heading for her office, Desire' racked her brain over and over again. She could not completely wrap her mind around the thoughts running rampant around her brain. Feeling defeated, Desire' plopped down in the chair and pulled up her email. Scanning her email, she decided there is no better way to get information than from the horse's mouth.

"Marie I thoroughly enjoyed our time at Happy Hour, something however has me quite concerned. Would you be interested in meeting me for brunch? I am a great cook at least I think so, LOL. My address is on the card. So I look forward to seeing you around eleven, Nik."

Feeling somewhat at ease, Desire headed for her small gym to burn more of the energy off that had her feeling like she was bouncing off the walls.

CONFESSIONS

Waking up the next morning Marie floated through her daily routine as if on a cloud. She began with an overly passionate kiss from Hilton, as he rushed out of the door headed to a morning meeting. Soon after his departure, Marie headed to her computer to check her emails and receive her morning inspiration. Noticing an urgent message from Nikki, Marie opened it first. Smiling to herself, she scanned the message. Marie quickly looked at the time and realized she had less than an hour to prepare. Responding to the message, Marie quickly typed, "See ya soon." As she began to close down the open emails, an instant message popped up. Seeing it was from her boss's personal account, Marie responded.

"Hi Cole, what's up?"

"Good Morning, I would like for you to accompany me to brunch, please!"

"Sorry Cole, but I already have plans."

"That's what you always say. Well, have fun beautiful."

Marie was not sure how to handle Cole and his constant advances yet. In the beginning they seemed quite harmless, yet now they were becoming more and more frequent. She knew she would definitely have to put an end to them and very soon.

A looming feeling suddenly overcame Marie as she stepped out of the shower. Knowing she was home alone she suddenly felt a creepy feeling down her spine. Turning around quickly and grabbing her robe, Marie headed to the keypad on the wall. Seeing that all the alarms were still engaged, she stood shaking her head, feeling quite hare-brained. Heading towards the bed, Marie heard the buzz of an instant message ring on her computer. Ignoring the buzz, Marie continued to dress as she cast an eye over to the clock on the night stand.

Continuing to dress, Marie was unaware that her every movement was being watched and recorded.

Putting the finishing touches on her fruit salad, Desire' pulled the premade quiche from the oven placing it on the cooling rack. Scanning the table display to ensure everything was perfect, she directed her attention to the centerpiece of stacked caramel and pecan glazed French toast. She hoped Marie was hungry; seeing that once again she had made way too much food. As she glanced at the time, Desire' headed over to the refrigerator to prepare the mimosa's and set the coffee maker up to brew.

Inspired by the morning motivational message coming from the radio, Desire knew she was making the right decision. Keeping her new friend was important to her and she was willing to do whatever it took. Beginning with a confession!

The knocking at the door brought Desire' out of her daze, as she glanced at the clock noticing it was eleven o'clock on the dot.

Opening the door, she smiled as Marie stood in the doorway yielding a huge bouquet of lilies and sunflowers. Seeing her surprise, Marie knew that she had made the correct selection.

"My Mother always told me never go to someone's house for the first time empty handed. Hope you like them, they are my favorites."

"Absolutely, see we have very similar taste, these are also my favorite flowers. I got some just last week from a friend. Where are my manners, please come in. I hope you brought your appetite, I always seem to overcook."

Seeing the table spread with Quiche, French toast with caramel and glazed pecans, blueberry scones, sausage, bacon and an array of fresh fruits, Marie turned to look at Nikki and replied, "You think."

The women again fell into laughter as they headed towards the delicious feast. Desire headed towards the refrigerator to retrieve the mimosa's she had just prepared with fresh squeezed juice. Pouring two flutes she sat down handing on to Marie, to new friends and a bright future. Clinking, the glasses and taking a sip the two women indulged in the food and conversation.

After consuming more than their stomachs could hold, the women sat contented at the table while continuing to have light hearted conversation. Sensing a change in the vibe in the room, Marie questioned, "Nikki is everything ok?"

Snapping out of her daze, Nikki stood and walked around the table taking a seat next to Marie. Sliding her chair in closer, she swallowed and knew there was no time like the present. Looking at her new friend, she felt a lump forming in her throat. As she opened her mouth to speak suddenly it felt dry as cotton. Apprehension was setting in, what if she didn't take the news well and wanted to fight her or worse? It would be easy to just keep the information she was about to share to herself, yet she knew her conscious would not allow her to maintain a real friendship under those circumstances. Taking a deep breath, Nikki exhaled and began to tell Marie the dreaded truth.

"You're married and your husband's last name is Scott?"

"Yes."

Feeling the rapid beating of her heart, Nikki continued. "Is his full name Hilton Jacob Scott?"

Looking puzzled and concerned Marie slid her seat back a little from Nikki and crossing her arms across her chest replied, "Yes" How did you know his name, I'm sorry that's a silly question. Is this about our kiss?

Nikki we both had a little too much to drink and I..."

Lifting her fingers to Marie's mouth she stopped her mid-sentence, "This is not about the kiss at Jalapeno's, it's much more and deeper than that. Please listen. If I don't say this now I won't be able to. Marie, I know Hilton on a personal level. My name is Nicole Desire' Riley. I met Hilton, three years ago while going through my divorce and until recently we were just friends. That was before I met you. We shared only one night of passion oral sex and I haven't actually seen him since. We've spoken and he should be arriving in a couple hours. We've had a late lunch every Monday for the past year. It wasn't until last night when I saw his truck in the driveway that I was able to connect the two names." Standing up and pacing back and forth in front of Marie, Nikki continued. "I never knew your name; Hill refers to you as his wife. From the way he talked I always assumed you were much older and going through something. He told me many times that you all hadn't had sex in something like five years. Hell, I even suggested he give you a week of daily surprises, I even picked out a red lingerie body suit from Adam & Eve. After he confessed that didn't work and you were not the least bit moved by the actions, I concluded you were not interested in saving your marriage. That night is when we engaged in congress, so to speak. I can't tell you I am sorry for that, because at the time I didn't know you." Stopping her constant pace, Nikki turned to look at Marie. The grimacing glare caused her to take a few steps back as Marie stood and walked to her.

Standing face to face with a woman who just admitted to sleeping with her husband, Marie was on fire. She looked at Nikki from head to toe. Slowly walking in a circle around her, Marie stopped behind her inhaled and walked back in front of Nikki. Face to face she could see the anxiety in Nikki as her rapid breathing increased. She looked as if she were going to faint. The moments seemed to tick away as the two women stood in the same place neither uttering a single word. The silence in the room thickened as Marie leaned forward, Desire stood in place bracing herself for what she assumed was about to happen. Inhaling her fragrance, Marie raised her hands, grabbing Nikki by the sides of her face with full palms and outstretched fingers. Unable to move, Nikki stood there with tears welling up inside her eyes as she knew that she had just lost a friend due to her confession. Seeing the look of panic spread across her face, Marie pulled Nikki closer with a forceful yank as she placed her open lips over Nikki's trembling mouth.

Nikki, felt the pounding of her own heart as she seemed to float above the scene playing out in her own dining room. Unable to control the feeling of anxiety, Nikki just stood there as Marie kissed her again with fierce desire. Pulling herself to reality, Nikki snatched away from Marie, still in shock she began to question her as tears streamed down her face. Unable to control the quiver in her voice "Did you understand what I just said? Why on earth are you kissing me again?" Aren't you the least bit angry?

Finding her voice, Marie stood there savoring the flavors of Nikki's mouth as she sat down smiling; she simply replied, "No, at least not with you!"

"Sit down, Nikki and let me explain something to you please. Relax. It's my own fault. I pushed Hill away time after time. We've been through a lot of things together. I sought therapy and nothing worked.   It wasn't until I met you at Jalapeno's that I was even able to make love to Hill. I am surprised he lasted as long as he did. I actually thought he had already slept with another woman. I installed a message tracer on his phone. I've seen the messages between him and a woman named Desire'. Shaking her head, she continued. "I just didn't know at the time the woman was you. Hill did send me the lingerie. It was kinkier than I usually liked and I pushed it aside, just as I had done his feelings. Please understand, I love my husband but after the birth of my son, I hadn't been able to make love to him. The night after meeting you I made love to him while images of you played behind my closed eyes. So how can I truly be mad at you when the predicament we are in begins with me? When we met a spark of fire ignited in me that I haven't felt in years. I want you Desire'. So here is a question for you, do you want to be with me and my husband?"

Sitting there with her mouth wide open in amazement, Nikki could not believe her ears! What in the hell has she gotten herself into. She couldn't believe Marie was sitting across from her, not angry or pissed, just horny and for to top it all off she wanted her to have a threesome with her husband. She was at a loss for words. She really couldn't believe the scene that had just taken place. Opening and closing her mouth several times, Nikki finally stood and began to pace the floor again. Looking back towards Marie, Nikki began to speak, but before she could get the words out, the ladies were startled by the sound of her door closing.

The unknown masked man, stood there clapping his hands at the ladies. Pointing the gun in their direction, Cole ordered the women to sit. Pulling the mask off his face, Cole looked at Marie and smiled.

"Of all the people you rejected me over, you choose her and Hilton. Well, now you're gonna pay and your bitch too!" Tossing the tape to Marie, Cole instructed her to strap Nikki down in the chair. Still startled, Marie stood and threw the tape back at Cole and began to speak.

"What the hell do you think you are doing, Cole? How many times have I told you I am not attracted to white boys, no matter how black you try to act?"

Seeing the resentment forming in his eyes, Cole raised the gun slightly and tossed the tape back to Marie.

"Do it now or I am gonna shoot the bitch, your choice darling."

Reluctantly Marie took the tape and began to wrap the tape around Nikki sitting in the chair. Leaning forward, she whispers, to her, "How long before you said, Hill comes for lunch?"

Looking at the clock, Nikki whispered, "One Hour."

Continuing to wrap the tape around Nikki; Marie stopped and looked at Cole. "What exactly do you want from me Cole?" She inquires.

With the gun still in hand, Cole points at Marie and with a sinister grin states, "Right now, strip."

Crossing her arms, defiantly Marie told Cole as long as Nikki is tied up my clothes stay on. Walking closer to her, Cole raises the gun at Marie. Staring straight into his eyes unmoving, Marie remained with her mouth tightly squeezed. Remove the tape and we will both strip for you, Cole or you can just shoot me now. Marie walked closer to Cole, fear raging throughout her body. However, she would not relent and put Nikki in even more danger. She was totally unaware that Cole had become her stalker and she would not have anyone hurt. Stepping closer to Cole's outstretched arm she eases her head directly in front of his gun.

Sitting in the chair unable to speak, Nikki's eyes grew wider as Marie stood looking down the barrel of the assailant's gun. As tears streamed down her face, she knew Marie was in danger and there was nothing she could do to protect her. Keeping her eyes glued on Marie, Nikki retrieved her cellphone from her pocket quietly. Pushing the send button and praying silently that Hilton answered; she held the phone on her side and moved the chair to capture Marie's attention. She looked down when Cole pointed the gun towards her and yelled "Shut up Bitch!" Hoping that he or Marie continued to talk she whimpered in the chair.

Suddenly Marie, yelled, "Don't call her a Bitch Cole. It's you, an armed man against two helpless women, so who is the bitch here?"

"Don't make me shoot you Marie, because I will. I am not a bitch, I'm a Man dammit."

Raising his other hand and coming down hard across Marie's face, he spat out, "Who is a bitch now!"

Turning her face back around, Marie twisted her mouth around and spit the blood out into Cole's face and replied, "You are Cole and a real man never hits a woman."

Hearing the conversation, over Desire's phone, confused Hilton screeched to a stop in front of Desire's house. Seeing his wife's car confirmed it was actually her, he heard over the phone, but the black escalade next to hers was unknown. Sending Desire's address to Chase via text he instructed him to come quickly as there was a situation taking place. Standing at the doorway, Hilton dialed 911 and tells the operator to send a unit. He left the phone on the banister with the 911 operator still on the line as he eased his key into the lock.

Easing the door slightly open, Hilton could hear his wife talking to a man who sounded like her boss. Eyeballing the room through the cracked door, Hilton spotted Nikki strapped to a chair with duct tape across her mouth. Pushing the door open at full blast, Hilton crashed into the room with stealth. Knocking Cole to the floor as a shot rang out from his gun; Hilton pummeled Cole in the face. Being a boxer, he continued to hit Cole with combination after combination, until blood flew from all areas of his face. Clobbering him with another punch to the face for good measure Hilton stood and began to apply measured kicks into Cole's abdomen and side. Hearing the crunch of ribs and screams of pain, Hilton continued his assault on Cole until being pulled back by Chase.

Coming out of haze of anger, Hilton quickly ran to Marie lying on the floor. Unable to breathe properly, he pulled Marie into his arms and called her name. Chase leaned over picking up the gun lying on the floor; he walked over to Nikki and removed the tape from her mouth. Feeling the sting of the tape, didn't stop her from calling out to Marie lying in Hilton's arms. She had not moved yet, as blood slowly flowed from her head. Hilton cried over and over, Marie wake up babe, wake up I need you. Slowly opening her eyes, Marie felt intense pain and confusion as the blinding lights caused her to close her eyes once again quickly. Finding her voice, all she could muster out was Nikki. Looking back in a state of confusion towards Desire', Hilton's eyes questioned what was happening as Chase untapped her and she fought the urge to rush towards Hilton and Marie.

NIKKI

Soothing comfort overrode the feelings of anxiety that possessed her just moments ago. Sitting there in the arms of an unknown man, being comforted eased Nikki's tensions slightly. As he whispered softly to Nikki that everything was going to be fine the steady stream of tears slowly faded. A million thoughts begin playing through her head, she could feel herself still shaken and scared, but slowly began to relax with every caress and sympathetically spoken word from his mouth. She watched as Hilton held onto and called Marie's name over and over prior to the paramedics arrived and after they began working on her head, He never released her hand. That loving touch sent shivers through her very being. He was still very much in love with her no matter how he tried to deny it.

She couldn't guide her eyes away from the sight. Wonderment grasped her very being, here was one man thinking that his world had come to an end and another was being led out in cuffs. Cole looked like an ordinary white boy. He wasn't strikingly handsome, but his looks now were borderline ugly. Hilton really did a number on his face. Nikki though to herself, "I can sympathize with him. He fell hard for a woman who he could never have. I fell too, not as deep to stalk him or do bodily harm, but I was in way too deep with Hilton. This thing has to end. I knew danger and danger knew me, but this was more than I had bargained for. Now as I am sitting here being consoled by a man whom I don't even know, yearning for the affection displayed before me, I feel lost.

As she watched the stretcher being rolled out, she suddenly snapped back to reality and her own desires. She lowered her head as the reality of her own circumstances came to light.

"I have settled for being a side-chick, because taking a chance at real love scared me. Deep down I knew this situation wasn't right, but all those lonely nights had gotten the best of me. Hilton lavished me with attention and gifts, things that made a woman feel special. It was all an illusion, moments of stolen lust. Real devotion and love is being played out right in front of my eyes. It is apparent that Hilton truly loves Marie, she is his soul-mate and I am his play-mate. Something I can no longer be. It is time for me, Nicole, to start living again. Time for me to get the real love that I know is in store for me."

IT JUST SO HAPPENS

As the police and paramedics entered into Nikki's house she began to explain the series of events that had taken place which led to Marie being led out on a stretcher and Cole in handcuffs. Sitting beside Chase, she told Hilton about her and Marie's meeting at Jalapeno's. Their brief meeting and subsequent friendly date for happy hour; as she continued to talk, the police, asked her had she known that they were being watched by Marie's boss Cole Blackwood III. Shaking her head in bewilderment, she had not even known Cole and was unaware of his presence in Marie's life. She had only known her friend for a short time.

Still shaken visibly Chase placed his arm around Nikki as Hilton held Marie's hand. The paramedic's had her on the stretcher strapped in with oxygen over her face. As they continued to work on her while heading out the front door, Hilton looked back at Desire' and lowered his head. Feeling as if he failed her, he followed his wife into the ambulance. Inside the ambulance, Marie finally able to speak, removed the oxygen mask and told Hilton, "I'm sorry please forgive me, but I need you to bring Desire' in here too.

MARIE

Being near death can certainly be an eye opener. Well I wasn't exactly dying but the thought has crossed my mind a time or two. It seemed as though I have made quite a huge mess of my life. From the outside everything looks absolutely perfect. But the truth is my life is far from it. I have been married to a man who placed me on a pedestal, he thinks I am the best wife and mother ever. However I am far from it. The secrets left untold from my life are coming back to haunt me. I can't say that I am surprised, considering Karma has a way of catching up to you. I just wasn't prepared. I still can't believe that night with Cole Blackwood would lead to almost losing my life. At some point in time I knew I would have to tell the truth to Hilton, but I didn't expect it to be so soon. How will I ever explain all of my misgivings without seeming like a common whore? I could possibly turn the tables and tell Hill it's his entire fault. He is the one who wanted to watch all the porn and sending all the sexist lingerie! Is it really my fault that I wanted to explore the lifestyle? I mean really, at first I was just checking out the scenes, something to add the spice back into my marriage. But soon it became an obsession.

The first party I attended I just stood in the corner and watched. I was not feeling it. Women with women, men with women and men, it was just a big ass orgy. I didn't want any part of it, but I couldn't turn my eyes away. I watched the women sex the women and then turn around and jump on a man like it was no big deal. I was fascinated with the whole thing. Yet it wasn't something I was sure I wanted to do. No, I couldn't see some other woman bent over being fucked by Hill while I suck on her tits. That just wasn't something I wanted to do, but the feelings that came from watching others intrigued me. I couldn't stop watching and listening. I should have left. No, I should have never gone in the first place. Marriage is sacred between man and woman. When you invite others into it, a mess can be made. I should have listened to my inner conscious. But when Cole Blackwood, walked in with a little Asian chic, I had to watch. At first I didn't know that he recognized me, I mean I had on platinum wig, oversized clothes and one of Hill's ball caps. But apparently that did little to hide who I was. Cole walked right up to me and whispered to me to watch and I did.

That night was the beginning of the end. I love my husband, really I do but he is not well endowed so to speak. When we married, I was still a virgin. I know that's hard to believe in this day and time, but my parents didn't play the radio. Having a Mother as a pastor is worse than having a father as a one. She was like *TD Jakes* in a skirt. Everything that I tried as a teen she was two steps ahead of me always. She was determined that I walk the straight and narrow. I could always remember her words, "You are not going to embarrass me little girl."

So that night changed everything I thought I was, I watched Cole. The rumor I always heard about white men having itty bitties was dispelled. Cole was hung like a horse. He was strapped up larger than my own husband. I was shocked and enthralled. I could not tear my eyes away. The Asian chic he was with couldn't hang. She barely had half of his girth inside her and she screamed in delightful torment. I think he put on that show for my sake. It was fascinating. I often wondered why he stopped so soon. But that is another story entirely. After that brief encounter, I returned to the same spot often. I never participated but I watched. Cole came several more times, and never with the same woman. No matter what disguise I wore he always knew it was me. He'd come over and always whisper *watch* and I did. I watched him and every woman that he came in with.

I wasn't attracted to Cole, but I enjoyed watching him fuck various women. I watched various other people as well.

Nothing prepared me for what I would end up watching unexpectedly in the sauna after working out at Beach Bodies one afternoon. That evening changed everything. I never returned to the spot and later informed Cole I had no intentions of ever sleeping with him. My mind was set on other things from that moment on.

"So you knew that this Cole, guy was digging you and you never spoke up about it?" Nikki asked.

"Yes but you see, Cole and I work together." "I never thought anything else about it after, I told him I wasn't interested." Marie replied.

"Oh I see, go ahead." Nikki stated.

Well what happened in the sauna changed my perspective of things. After spending a couple of hours working out, I retreated to the sauna to let the steam soak away some of the stress I had compounded myself with. There was no one in the sauna that night and the gym was almost empty, so I lay there in silence with only my thoughts to keep me company. The lights were dimmed and the steam was slowly beginning to make my body relax. As I was starting to drift off, the door eased open slightly. I didn't open my eyes, to look I just figured it was another woman entering to do the same thing I was doing. Then the hushed whispers aroused my thoughts. So I rolled over slightly to see who had entered and almost fell off the bench when my eyes focused in on what was going on. I was shocked, and laid there extremely still watching the scene unfold before my eyes. There were two women; I couldn't quite make out their faces as they were buried within each other and standing in front of them giving instructions was Chase.

"Hold up, is that the same Chase, I rode here to the hospital with?" Nikki inquired.

"Yes." Marie uttered while trying to adjust herself in the bed.

She examined Nikki's facial expressions even more at the mention of Chase. It seemed to her that she was intrigued, like many women when they first meet him.

"So what happened next, did they see you?" Nikki asked.

No, none of the freaky threesome even noticed I was there. They were busy pleasuring themselves. Chase was enjoying himself, giving the women orders telling them which way to turn, how to suck each other's nipples and where to touch. Then suddenly, the door opened again and she strolled in, the mystery lady was wearing a red leather cat suit, kinda exactly like the one that Hill sent me. She had thigh high boots and a medium sized bag on her shoulder.

Everyone froze in place, including me. My breathing intensified tremendously. I've never seen a woman control Chase, but she did. The two women who were answering his every command sat stark still with their backs arched and hands placed on their knees. I could see their breast rise and fall in calm self-possessed unison. The mystery woman walked straight up to Chase as he immediately fell to his knees. I could barely see her face, but I could hear her voice loud and clear. She ordered him to kiss her feet and immediately he did as instructed, just as the two women had before.

"Wait a minute, are you really telling me that Chase, was being subservient to this mystery woman?"

"That's exactly what I am saying," Marie replied.

"Okay so what happened next?" Nikki said.

I wanted to move closer to get a better view of the scene taking place right before my eyes but without being noticed. After she gave a Chase a couple more orders, she blind folded him and directed the girls to proceed out the sauna. I was a tad bit disappointed that the show was ending. I let out a sigh just a little too loud. She stopped in her tracks and turned in my direction. A shallow laugh escaped her mouth as she back tracked her steps and headed in my direction. She stopped, looking back towards the entrance way and then walked straight up to me. She leaned in where I was laying I could smell her minty breath she was so close. Examining my face with squinted eyes, she whispered in my ear, "My shows are private pretty girl; I'll make an exception this time. Next time you pay to play."

"Does Chase know you are here?"

I couldn't speak. I was cold busted, so I just nodded my head, no. Her next move caused me to jump off the bench, as her tongue traced the bottom lobe of my ear her hand cupped my exposed breast. I begin to back up, but was stopped by the bench.

Seeing the shock on my face, a crooked smile eased up the side of her mouth. "You're a newbie!" she said. I don't do newbie's." She said, placing her hands on my shoulders.

The simple act of control sent shivers down my spine. She must've felt my shudder. Sit down, she commanded. It was something about the way she spoke that made me sit straight down on the bench. I stood back up quickly, she laughed. With the one hand still placed on my left shoulder, she gently slid down the length of my arm, caressing it little by little. When she reached my palm, I was totally relaxed. Her thumb circled my wedding rings, as she opened her mouth to ask, I said twelve years before the question ever came out.

"Your first?" she replied. I nodded.

Then that crooked smile appeared again on her full mouth.

She said, "You want to do this with your husband?"

I started to nod again, when she dropped my hand leaning into my face she spoke. I could feel the air coming from her minty breath, but there was a hint of something else. Another scent, I couldn't quite make out. Her voice was not commanding as before it was just slightly above a whisper and seductively she uttered two words, "Say it."

"Yes", I replied over and over.

As she leaned back from my face her eyes roamed my body. I pulled the towel up closer and that crooked smile appeared on her face once again. The electricity passing through me continued and the hairs on my arms stood up. Her eyes peered at me, they seemed to change colors right before me. I blinked a couple of times and refocused. The longer she looked at me, the lighter her eyes appeared; they went from a black midnight hue to almost hazel. When she opened her mouth to speak her eyes once again were midnight black.

"I can make your fantasies come true," she said.

I opened my mouth to protest what she was saying but she quickly placed a single raised finger on my mouth.

She proceed, "Don't waste my time pretty girl; I know every single fantasy you have. You've been watching couples have sex, a white boy in particular. But you're not interested in him, the women he fucks fascinate you. You want to have a threesome with your husband. You want to control the man, like I controlled Chase moments ago."

My mouth dropped open! I couldn't utter a single word. The thoughts running through my mind were rampant.

She smiled that crooked grin again and said, "You will meet the woman who is going to change your naïve thinking. You have two choices, before anything occurs. You can keep the life you have or you can enter the life you think you want. Once you step through either door, however you can't go back. You want to be a bad pretty girl but that's not what the good reverend raised. Choose wisely pretty girl and we will meet again."

At that, she turned and walked out the sauna leaving me there alone with all the thoughts inflicting havoc on my brain.

"Two days later, I met you Nikki. I couldn't get you out of my mind. There was that same electricity coursing through me, when we shook hands. I had no idea that you also were the woman, that my husband was spending time with. I read the text he sent and received from Desire, but when we met you introduced yourself as Nikki D. Riley. I didn't make the connection, how could I. The numbers were different and I never saw a picture of your face."

"Marie, let me explain." Nikki said.

"There's no explanation needed. Hilton is and was feeling you. I must admit that after we met, I was too. Now I just don't know." Marie replied.

"No you have to listen, it really wasn't like that. See we were just friends; we talked and enjoyed some of the same things. I had no intentions of being anything more or less than friends." Nikki said.

"You told me at brunch, Nikki. It's understandable, Hilton is a desirable man." Marie replied, "But we can discuss that later. I have a proposition for you to consider. But first I am sure Hilton wants to know what we are talking about for so long." Marie said.

HILTON

Pacing the floor outside of her room, Hilton wondered what in the hell were they talking about for so long. He cringed at the fact that maybe his Desire was telling his wife every sordid detail of their beginning affair. This can't be happening he thought to himself. How does my wife and my girlfriend end up being friends. This kinda shit only happens in movies. He reasoned. Trying to make sense of the entire fiasco he continued to pace up and down the hall. He spotted Chase walking back up towards, He tried to calm himself. Get it together Hilton, he admonished himself. Maybe they are just going over what happened with that punk ass Cole. As Chase approached, Hilton exhaled his frustrations and put on his game face.

"You can save that look for your wife and girlfriend," Chase said. I know you Hill.

"How in the hell does your side chic and wife become close friends?"

"Your guess is as good as mine!"

"You know I love Marie, like a little sister, Chase replied. "But shorty is fine as a motherfucker, what did you say her name was?"

"Desire."

"That's her real name? Bro," Chase inquired.

"Yeah, it's Nicole Desire Riley," Hilton replied.

"You been holding out on ya boy Hill, that ain't even cool. Where did you meet her, shit she gotta sister?"

"Naw man, she's an only child and I wasn't holding out on you. I was actually going to introduce you to her. I thought she could straighten yo ass out. But then I don't know things changed. Marie wasn't letting up with the arguing and she was still distant. I started talking to Desire more and more. We bonded. She just filled in the spaces that Marie left deserted."

"Damn man, I wish you would have?" "Did you hit it?" Chase asked

Breathing heavily, Hilton replied, "No I didn't hit, but she does taste like a sweet Georgia peach."

"Peach, um I could eat a peach all day!" Chase replied.

"You got jokes, I see." Hilton chuckled.

Before the conversation continued, the room door eased open as Nikki walked out and the nurse walked in. She looked a bit tired, as we all did. But even with the red eyes and slight bags, she was still attractive to Chase. He rushed to her offering his hand leading her to the open seat. Hilton stood there watching the transaction with his mouth agape. He couldn't believe how chivalrous Chase was being. Before he could open his mouth to utter something to either of them, the Nurse walked back out of Marie's room.

"Mr. Scott, your wife wants to see you now and only for a few minutes. The doctor will be in shortly," she said.

Taking a deep breath Hilton; glanced back at Chase and Desire sitting quite close to one another. Desire sat looking at Chase intensely as they engaged in light conversation.   Chase suddenly sprang up from his seat and walked over to Hilton.

"I am going to take Desire to the cafeteria, get some coffee. Do you want something?" Chase asked.

"Looks like you want to take her to more than the cafeteria." Hilton responded.

The look on his face at that moment, made Chase step in closer as he lowered his voice.

"Look man, I just don't want the lady to feel like sloppy seconds. You have more than enough problems to deal with and you haven't even said two words to her since we got here." Chase said. "If you got a problem with that, I will back off."

"Naw, I'm tripping Chase, go ahead, she is a wonderful woman and besides I have to try and save my marriage. I just hope that I haven't sent myself to divorce court." Hilton replied.

"Go check on your wife, I got Ms. Desire. She's in good hands; you know I am like Allstate."

"I see you still got jokes, Hilton replied before turning and opening the door.

Walking into his wife's room, Hilton didn't know what to do or say. He smiled relieved that she was awake and sitting up. That however was short lived when he saw the look on her face. Slowly he walked over to her bedside trying to muster up the words to say. He knew that look so very well. In the past, an argument would definitely ensue. However at this very moment the last thing he wanted was an argument. Breathing deeply, he dropped down to his knees and reached for her hand.

Sliding her hand away slightly, Marie gazed in Hilton's eyes. She tried to read his expression, but came up with nothing more than sorrow. Exhaling deeply, she whispered, "Hill stand up, there is no need for you to be on the floor."

Before he could speak, the doctor walked back into the room accompanied by the nurse from before. Hilton moved to the other side of the bed, and took possession of Marie's hand. Listening to the doctor speak, he caressed her cold hand beneath his.

"Mrs. Scott good news, we will be able to release you today. I implore you take it lightly for the next couple of weeks. The nurse has your discharge papers and will process you out shortly. I suggest you follow up with your primary doctor in a week."

The news of her release from the hospital brought the first smile to Marie's face. Hilton hadn't seen her smile in months and a tear threatened to fall as he released her hand to shake hands with the doctor.

BEHIND CLOSED DOORS

After being released from the hospital, Marie spent the next few days withdrawn and bedridden. She had been feeling that all the events that transpired were her fault and she couldn't bring herself to face the one person who desperately wanted answers. She had spent two days in the hospital for observation. Although she thought she had been shot by Cole, she hadn't. The gash on her forehead had come from hitting the corner of Nikki's end table. Hilton, Nikki and Chase had stayed with her the entire two days. She faded in and out of consciousness during her first night's hospital stay. But each time she awoke, Hilton was stationed on one side and Nikki on the other.

On the second day, she was able to speak with Nikki and the confession began. However she had yet to explain anything to Hilton. Avoidance wasn't working and she knew in her heart she had some major explaining to do.

Pulling the covers back up over her head, Marie wished for death to come swiftly and take her. She never wanted to bring pain to anyone or to herself for that matter. But the fact still remained, regardless of how she tried to hide it, cover it up or just plain forget about it. She was the source of all this mess. She felt that telling Hilton the details would lead to divorce. Was she really ready to take that road? Trying her best to rationalize the events leading up to Cole becoming her stalker would not be easy to tell Hilton.

Sitting back in the bed, the tears began to stream down her eyes again. She buried her head into the pillow and screamed one more time. She had enough. Crying made her feel weak for no apparent reason. Easing off the bed, Marie made her way into the shower.

Thinking about how to approach the conversation with Hilton was no easy task and she needed a clear head. Stepping into the steamy spray, she stood there for what seemed like hours letting the events of the previous days and weeks play through her head. How could she tell Hilton of all the things she had done without losing him. Could she possibly not tell him? As the hot spray grew colder, Marie stepped out the shower and grabbed a towel. Walking back into the room, she stopped dead in her tracks at the sight of Hilton sitting on the bed reading her journal. Her heart sank into her feet as her eyes fixated on Hilton's as he rose up off the bed.

"Hilton, I can explain." Marie started.

"Explain, explain. How in the hell can you explain what I just read? Huh?"

"First of all Hilton, lower your voice when talking to me there's no need to shout, the kids might hear you."

"I sent them to your mothers. I have been waiting on you to wake up before I came in Marie." Hilton replied.

"There's still no reason to yell, Hill I said I can explain."

"It's all here in black and white; what can you explain." "How my wife has been running around town acting like a common whore." "Did you fuck him?" "Is that why I can't get it? Huh?"

"You got me around here scratching my head, bending my ass over backwards to try and please you and all the while you're playing office whore?"

Closing the space between them, Marie dropped the damp towel, she was holding on to on the floor. With a bowed head, she let a single tear fall from her eyes before lifting up to peer into Hilton's contorted face.

"You will not call me another whore as long as you plan to be my husband, Hilton."

"I've never slept with anyone other than you. And you will not disrespect me. Remember you are not innocent in this entire fiasco." "Or have you forgotten about Desire?" Marie stated.

"Are you serious, Marie? You really want to blame Desire for this?" She doesn't even know Cole. "You do! Hilton bellowed."

"And you're right, but I didn't sleep with Cole, can you say the same about Desire?" "I don't want to fight Hilton, let me explain please. There is more than what you read. Besides, I think you have a bit of explaining to do yourself. Nikki, I mean Desire told me everything about you and her."

"What about me and her? You know what it doesn't matter, because if you had spent some time taking care of me, I would have never turned to another woman. I love you. I have tried over and over to show you just how much you mean to me. But what happened nothing. Now I know why nothing happened between us. I now know why the spark has left our life. You were too busy shaking and showing your damn ass to everybody else. All I wanted was to be a good husband. You women are a damn trip; you say you want a good man, a real man, a man to provide everything you need. Well damn I did all that for you but did you appreciate me? Hell no. You pushed me away. You rejected me over and over, and now you want to be surprised that I ended up in another woman's bed?" Hilton exclaimed. "Well fuck it, you want to know something; I should've fucked her and every other woman that threw themselves at me."

"Hilton please, I know you fucked someone else!" Marie yelled back.

"It's been 5 years since we've made love. Do you really expect me to believe you didn't fuck someone else that whole while?" "Come on man, I was born at night, not last night! Marie slurred.

"Don't you see I have what I always wanted?   I married the woman of my dreams!"

"Yeah Hilton, what about your fantasies, huh? The truth is YOU started this! Let's do something new, watch a movie, put this on, and put that on. You have no idea how I wanted to tell you about this burning flame laying deep within. Only problem is, I never really understood it until I met Nikki, I mean your Desire. Hill will you please just let me explain, please baby give me a chance."

Hilton shaking his head didn't wanna hear the bullshit coming out of his wife's mouth but the mention of Desire still had his nose wide open, he couldn't help but listen. He sat back down on the bed and said, "Go ahead, Marie explain why for the last five fucking years I gave you my everything and you gave me nothing but blue balls and treated me as if I was the some disease infested creature you couldn't bear to be around, go right ahead, I can't wait to hear this shit. Marie took a deep breath and said to herself: "here goes nothing."

"Well everything you said is true. I was wrong. I was so caught up in this dream world that my reality never crossed my mind. My very own Pandora's Box was open and frankly I didn't know what to do with it. Hill, I love you more than anything and I would never do anything to hurt you intentionally. I just thought until I figured out what was wrong with me and this sexual fetish, demon, I don't know whatever it is, I might as well love you from a distance so I wouldn't hurt you. But I hurt you anyway. I love watching people have sex. It turns me on in a way I never felt before until I met Desire. Something about that woman has me so wide open. I know you know what I am talking about because you have that same feeling for her. It's like you just wanna take her all in."

"So what Marie, are you telling me you're gay now?"

"No Hill, I am not. I am a woman who loves her husband more than anything and is intrigued with the filthy fetishes. You know what, I wanna show you. I been so embarrassed baby, please just go with me and maybe you can understand what I mean. Will you please go Hill, please I don't wanna lose you and I am trying to show you why I have been so torn."

Hilton could see the embarrassment and yet the deep longing for something more in Marie's eyes. Although he was angry and hurt, he knew he loved her way to much to let something like this come between them. "Get dressed, let's go."

Although Marie hadn't been to the sex club in a while, once she entered the doors all her sexual arousals became to wake up. She watched Hilton intensely as they made their way to a corner so they can get their look on. "Hill, I swear on my life I have never engaged in any of these activities, I have only watched." Not knowing what to believe at this point, Hilton simply said, "Yeah, ok, whatever you say."

Marie was right. This was some freaky shit. Hilton had never felt as sexually free as he did right now. It was amazing to watch people have open sex with one another. It was a real life porn movie. There were girls on girls, men with women with other women. People watching, damn folks were cheering on blowjobs and anal sex. He had to admit, his dick was getting hard as fuck and his sexual appetite was in overdrive. He tried to regroup and focus on Marie. He could see in her face that she was in sexual bliss. He was wondering if she was about to have an orgasm without being touched when all of a sudden Chase came in the door.

"OMG, Marie look, its Chase. What the fuck is he doing here?"

"Hill, I told you, you don't know what people sexual secrets are. Look he just joined in without hesitation."

Hilton's mouth was wide open. My boy Chase never told me about this side of him. I knew he was a freak and loved the ladies but damn, I didn't know he got down like this. Look at my boy go. That's my nigga right there beating somebody's pussy up. Hilton couldn't help but laugh as he continued to scan the room to see if he recognized anyone else. Not bad, not bad at all, I just wish Marie could have trusted me to let me in on her life, this is something we could have been sharing together, shit who knows we might have been able to participate. Naw, I never wanted to share her with anyone thinking I love her too much as he grabbed her and pulled her close.

With that simple move, Marie knew she had him right where she wanted. "Hill baby, take me home and fuck the shit out of me, I been a naughty girl and I need to be punished."

"Word, it's like that? Let's go."

With that, Marie and Hilton exited the club and went home to rekindle the fire that had burned out. Hilton immediately put his hand up Marie's skirt and started fingering with her pussy. Damn it felt so good to have his wife again.

Before they were around the block good Marie looked at Hilton and said, "Fuck me now!" Marie spread her legs open further and grabbed Hilton's hand so he could take his fingers deeper into her now soaking wet pussy.

Hilton wasted no time pulling the car over in a shaded area so he could make love to his beautiful wife, the woman of his dreams. As soon as the car can to a complete stop, Marie mounted Hilton in one leap. She pulled his dick out got on top and began to ride like there was no tomorrow. Hilton was so far gone with admiration for his wife a tear began to fall. He had been waiting for five years to get this Marie back and he wasn't going to do anything to mess it up.

As Marie worked her cunt up and down Hilton's dick, she closed her eyes and was thankful that her husband had forgiven her and was still in love with her. With each up and down motion and his dick going deeper and deeper in her Marie began a series of mini orgasms which was causing her to lose control. Breathing heavily and closing her eyes she began to see Desire in this most intimate moment. She was riding Hilton's dick with force and speed and he was in pure ecstasy.

With every thrust, Marie closed her eyes and saw Desire. "OMG, OMG, I wanna cumm. Baby I wanna cumm. I wanna fuck you and Desire!!"

Oh no, no I didn't just say that Marie thought as she exploded with the thought of tasting Desire and watching her fuck and suck her husband.

Did Hilton just hear her right? Did she say she wanted to fuck me and Desire? With those words and thinking about how wonderful the taste of Desire's pussy was and how powerful his wife's grip on his dick was, he exploded deep within her pussy as she fell forward on him and he let the seat back as far as it would go.

With both of them breathing heavily, Marie opened her eyes and looked dead into Hilton's eyes and said, "I wanna fuck Desire. I wanna taste her, I wanna watch while you fuck her. I want to have a threesome with the two of you because at the end of the day, I am strongly attracted to her and I know you are too. We both win if you agree."

Hilton was amazed at the boldness he was getting from Marie. He was actually more turned on than ever before. The thought of eating his wife's pussy and

Desire's pussy had his dick at attention. My wife wanted to taste my Desire's pussy. And I get to fuck her; this was a win for the both of them.

"Marie I love you more than life and if this is what you truly want, I will do it. Now let's go home. I wanna make love to my beautiful wife." Marie smiled and rubbed Hilton's dick all the way home. She was finally going to get what she wanted now all she had to do was convince Desire. I'm sure that won't be a problem I know she wants to fuck my husband and I know she wants to fuck me so doing a threesome should be easy, Marie thought to herself as she noticed the grin on her husband's face.

DESIRE

Desire hung up the phone with Marie wondering what was so important that it couldn't wait till the morning. After all she only had been out the hospital a few days. Never the less Marie was on her way over and she needed to take a quick shower and freshen up a bet. Truth be told, she definitely was excited about seeing Marie. Ever since Marie told her about her secret, Desire's world really had changed a lot. For started, she had been having a serious fling with Chase. Desire smiled as she pulled her outfit together and laid it on her bed so she could go hop in the shower.

Chase had taken Desire home from the hospital. He was so friendly and concerned about her it kind of happened by Chase. Laughing to herself as she lathered her Shea Butter body wash on her loofah, Desire remembers their first sexual encounter.

Chase came inside with Desire, because truthfully she was still a little shook up from everything that had taken place in her home. Chase was very soft spoken and attentive. He made Desire some tea and told her to rest for a bit while he cleaned up a little.

"That's not necessary Chase, I can take care of it." Desire said, and started removing broken picture frames and items from her floor.

"Listen pretty lady, you have been through a lot too, your house damn near got destroyed and on top of all that, Hilton told me a little bit about your history with him." Chase said, as he handed her a cup of tea.

"Oh, he told you uh? Well I am probably not a person you need to waste your time around, I am so embarrassed." Desire said holding her head down.

Chase sat next to her and lifted her head up slowly and said, "Don't hold your head down. You are a beautiful woman and you cannot help if a married man or shit, hell any man in general was attracted to you. I mean Hill is a good dude. I am sure he never had any intentions of hurting you. Hey look at the outcome... You met me." Chuckling to himself, he continued with his make me feel better speech.

'Anyways, Ms. Desire, you are so much better than being the other woman. You are the only woman material. Chin up, now what else can I get you, would you like me to make you a sandwich or something.' Chase said walking toward the kitchen like he lived there and really was all about pleasing me. I smiled.

"Sure why not, I have some lunch meat in the fridge and bread in the pantry. I can do that myself you know. I mean you're my guest in my house and yet you are catering to me. How does that happen?" I said.

Poking his head out the kitchen, Chase smiled and said, "You're right, get your ass in this kitchen and fix me some food woman." Then he cranked up and said, 'Girl, don't look all crazy, it was a joke. I don't mind. I never really spent any quality time with a woman. If it wasn't about the booty, I never cared so this is a change of pace for me.'

Chase brought me the sandwich and a glass of lemonade. He sat down and we had a really awesome conversation. It was like we knew each other our entire life. We shared everything. I told him about the kiss with Marie and the oral satisfaction from Hilton. I also told him about my failed marriage, the hurt, and pain that I struggled with on a regular. Surprisingly he was an open book with me. He told me he was a ladies man of the sort. He even told me about the sex rooms, chats, and dominatrix was involved with. He had such a sincere disposition and openness about himself; I guess everything else was automatic.

Our bodies were like magnets on each other. It was like he was exactly what I needed and I know I met all his expectations of a quality woman that night. For that night, I was his Desire and he was mine. Our bodies intertwined and we never missed a beat as we made deep passionate love. Yes it was love momentarily. Reminiscing on his stroke game Desire placed her hand in between her legs so she could touch her kitty. With the water flowing and the memory of Chase, it wasn't hard for Desire to bring herself to an orgasm. As she opened her eyes from her orgasm, she saw Marie standing in the bathroom staring it her.

"OMG, I didn't hear the doorbell." Desire was shocked and embarrassed, she hurriedly turned the water off and grabbed a towel all the while Marie never took her eyes off her which was turning Desire on in some strange way.

"Um, I rang the bell and when you didn't answer, I used Hilton's key." Marie said, in a sarcastic voice.

"Oh, ok, I forgot about that key.' Desire said, as she dried off and wrapped the towel around her body tighter. She grabbed the lotion and continued speaking while walking into the bedroom.

"Marie, I am sorry, as I told you before, I didn't know who you were and I know."

Before she could finish Marie said, "Desire I told you in the hospital we all do things we are not proud of and after all, Hilton is a very attractive man and anyways he knows he is married so regardless, this could never be your fault. All is forgiven. Here let me lotion you're back or something for you. Let's forget about all that."

"So I scarred you huh?' Marie said, grabbing the lotion from me as, I walked by heading to my bedroom.

"Looks to me like you were really enjoying yourself, who were you thinking about? Seems like whoever he or she was, had you transfixed in the moment."

Desire was trying to not focus on that question. She was desperately trying not to drop her towel and show anymore of her goodies. Marie was staring at her so intensely it kind of made Desire a little nervous but at the same time the lust in Marie eyes had her tingling and wondering what was to happen next. Sitting on the bed, crossing her legs Desire finally said, "Ha ha very funny, who says it has to be someone, I am so embarrassed."

"Girl please, stop that, everybody does it. Turn around so I can lotion your back good. You know you got to lower that towel so I can do the entire back. Or do you just wanna have moist shoulders and an ashy ass back."

"Really, I see you came with the jokes. Did you need someone to try your jokes out on? You know they'll bring Apollo back, if you audition, I promise I will not boo you off stage. Mmm, that feels good."

"Would you like a massage, lay down, I am an excellent masseuse. Chase taught me several reflexology techniques, I use them on Hilton well at least I used to."

Desire hesitated for a moment. Why is Marie here? What is her agenda? Damn her fingers are magical. One massage won't hurt, hell she already saw me naked and masturbating. Desire was willing and Marie was ready. Desire lay down on her stomach and loosened her towel. Marie removed the towel and mounted her pulling her own dress up high. She lowered her bare pussy slowly sitting right on top of Desire's ass and started a slow grind while rubbing Desire's back never missing a beat.

Desire finally spoke saying, "So this is really going to happen huh?"

"You know we have unfinished business. I wanted you since we met. I want you more now than I did then. If you want me to stop, say it."

"Umm, no it's ok." Desire said as she voluntarily turns over exposing her nakedness.

"I never thought I would say this too a woman, but I want you too Marie."

Marie bent down and slowly kissed Desire on the lips and this time, Desire reciprocated the kiss in a strong forceful way. The kiss was so passionate and so uninhibited that Marie immediately got so turned on she could feel her juices starting to course. She didn't know what to do so she did what came naturally.

She stood up and pulled her dress over her head. Desire thought Marie was the most beautiful woman she ever seen. It was hard to believe she ever had a kid in life she was everything a man looked for in a woman and the way Desire's clit was thrashing, obviously women liked also. No wonder Hilton never cheated on her in those five years. He had a goddess of his own. Hilton was right, Marie was gorgeous and she knew it. Her cockiness seeped through her skin and glistened.

Marie watched Desire lick her lips and couldn't help but to get turned on even more. Desire was so sexy. Everything about her screamed, fuck me and fall in love. She couldn't wait to taste her. She was her one desire and tonight she would satisfy that appetite. Marie's fantasy was coming true and it was all going down now.

Desire grabbed Marie by the hand and lowered her back to the bed. Slow intimate kisses over each other's body had them moaning. The sexual tension in the room had taken effect and Marie had placed her finger on Desire's now engorge clit rubbing and inserting another in her now soak pussy..

"Mmmmm." Desire was now opening her legs wider and Marie was grinding their pussies together, while finger fucking and kissing her at the same damn time. Desire continued letting out small moans of pleasure as Marie finger fucked and grind on her mound. Desire was overwhelmed with pleasure when Marie started her descend downtown for the first time ever. She slowly inserted her finger back in and spread Desire's legs and pussy lips open. Shivers came almost instantly.

The sensation of Marie's tongue making contact with the swollen folds; then her tongue making contact with her clitoris, Desire's entire body quivered. This was just the beginning as Desire experienced her first orgasm a couple of minutes later. Moans signaled Desire was enjoying herself and her moans got louder indicating she was cuming also. There's no faking the ejaculation of love honey which Desire sprayed on Marie's face. Smiling, Marie lifted her head licking her lips and said, "Mmm that was everything I thought it would be. You taste so good."

"Let me taste you, sit on my face. I can't wait." Desire said to Marie.

Marie couldn't wait. Her pussy was dripping wet as she lowered her pussy unto Desire's waiting lips. Marie almost came instantly with Desire's first two licks. Marie began to moan and gasp just like Desire did a few minutes before. Marie moaned loudly as her love juices exploded in Desire's mouth. Desire sucked all the juices out of her pussy and as Marie's body did slow jerks as she slowly removed herself from Desire's mouth and replaced her pussy with her tongue in Desire's mouth. Desire stuck two fingers up her pussy as Marie sat on top of her, gyrating her body and kissing her deeply.

The two women continued until they both fell backwards from the orgasm they shared together. Exhausted and still excited they shared one more kiss before either one of them spoke.

"Now I know why my husband was so addicted to you. I mean I knew there was something distinctive about you the first time I met you but I never thought it would be this good. I can't believe I cheated on my husband and then with a woman."

"Do you regret it Marie? I'm sorry, I knew this was a bad idea, I don't know what is going on in my head lately. I, I, I am so sorry." Desire said, as she was rushing to get up to get dressed feeling real embarrassed.

"Calm down Nikki, I mean really, I wanted this way more than you will ever know. What I meant by that was I didn't come over here for this reason. I mean I saw you in the shower playing with yourself and got so turned on I couldn't help it. I'm so sorry if I made you feel bad, please come back to bed." Marie said, tugging at Desire's arm.

Desire sat down on the bed and said, "I can't believe that we just....I actually was with you. I really did have a great time, oh, why did you come over?"

"Um, well I wanted to talk to you about Hilton. I know you were really feeling him. I read his journal. He was really feeling you also. I neglected my husband and I can't blame anyone for anything that happened but me. I wanted to talk to you about doing me a favor."

"You know I am your friend and I will do anything for you. What do you need ReRe. You mean a lot to me and I don't wanna loose our friendship. What can I do?"

Marie took both of Desire's hands in hers and looked her dead in the eyes and said, "Fuck my husband and me."

"What, are you high? A threesome, are you serious?"

"Desire, we love you. We both want you. What we just did was beautiful. I am never going to forget this ever. But, you know you wanna fuck my husband. If you had not put two and two together, you would have fucked him without hesitation already. Well I am giving you permission to sleep with Hill. I don't wanna give you up. He will drop you like a bad habit if he thinks your friendship will cause conflict with me and him. I love my husband and he loves me but the contentment he found in you, I can never change and all the trouble I put him through, he deserves to have his DESIRE. I mean I got to have you. I already gave him permission. He knows I wanna fuck you and I asked him if we could do a threesome and he said yes. That alone, lets me know he still wants you."

"Now I am not saying this is going to last forever but what I feel for you is so strong and what Hilton feels for you is even stronger. I know you feel the same way. I could feel it when you touched me."

Marie grabbed Desire's face and stuck her tongue down her throat and kissed her so long and deep. Desire almost forgot the question that was just proposed to her. Pushing Marie away, she caught her breath and tried to speak, but Marie was too swift, she pushed her back on the bed taking her feet into her hand, she began applying slow steady pressure to her gonad area between the heel and arch. Massaging the area in slow circular motions, Marie began to speak.

"Desire, please fuck me and my husband. Say it, say your desire is a ménage a trios, say it."

She was in a daze. Her pussy started tingling with pleasure and without another thought, just as she felt her juices erupt, she uttered the words, "Yes, yes I will."

CHASE

It's true what they said about once you find the right woman it will change your life. Nikki was just that woman. I mean I was instantly attracted to her but once we sat down and actually talked, it was a wrap. Yep, I am thinking about throwing in the towel with all other women. She might be the one, Chase thought to himself as he waited for his man Hilton to come through.

Chase hadn't really spoken with Hilton since the hospital. Thinking back, that was some wild ass shit that went down. Who would have thought Marie would go this far or get in that deep. Guess you never really know anyone. Shit look at me. Lost in daydreams of his *Desire*, Chase thought to himself, damn I don't know how I am going to tell Hilton; Nikki and I are an item or real close to it. That shit shouldn't mean a damn thing, he is married and he ain't leaving his wife for no one so as far as I am concerned, his Desire has now been confirmed as my Desire, better luck next time, Chase thought with a crazy ass grin on his face. Just the thought of her had his dick on rock. She had good pussy and those lips were too addictive. She was the sweetest most loving person he ever met and Chase fully intended on telling her just that later tonight or maybe he would just show her.

"Bro, why you got that cheesy ass grin on your face? What you trying to get into? Or better yet *who* you trying to get in to? "Hilton said as he sat down. 'What's up with you thanks for meeting me.'

Chase responded with, "What's good with you Mr. Hilton? You know me, everything is everything. I am living every man's dream. How are things with you, Marie, the kids, everybody good?"

"Man the kids are great, growing like weeds, you know how that goes. I'm good.

Business is good, profits are great. And Marie, well that's a whole other subject; you might not even have enough time left on his earth to comprehend what goes on in her head. But she is doing well and is back to her normal self. She is sexing me and everything."

"Say word? Damn, what the fuck got into her. Just like that, I mean a 360; guess a near death experience changes a mofo lifestyle for real. Congrats man I know how that drought had your mind warped. Let me guess, she put the smack down on that dick didn't she? Hell yeah, I can see that shit all over your face, I ain't mad at cha."

Laughing at his friend, Hilton shook his head and replied," Man, baby girl got her freak straight on. Dawg, we fucked in the car." Chase looked shocked as hell as Hilton continued.

"Man, I found Marie's journal and I read it. Yes, I see your face but I was tired. I needed answers. I wanted to know what the fuck was going on with my wife. Five years is a long time to hold out on someone. Anyways, she has been an undercover freak. Not fucking all over the place but dude, my wife is into fetishes. She had been watching folks having sex. She's a damn voyeur. She likes watching other people have sex. That's why Cole was stalking her and shit. She has been at the sex clubs and stuff watching him fuck women."

Hilton took a sip of water and coughed then continued, "By the way, she wrote that she seen you a couple times at the freak house, man I am not even gonna ask, just hope you used protection."

"Wow! What the hell she writing that shit in a diary for? What else did she say about me?" Chase nervously asked.

"Nothing, just that she seen you getting your freak on with some chick. Oh she also said that you had the smallest Johnson in the world.

"Shit, I doubt that. If anything, she said that a nigga got a king dong and I wish my Hilton had that. Then maybe, I would fuck him again instead of watch his king dong friend."

"Yeah, haha, I see you got jokes. Everybody wanna be Kevin Hart. Can I finish my story or are you gonna clown."

"Oh my bad, go ahead tell me everything." Silently thanking the good man above that was all Marie wrote about him.

"Anyways, she fucked me silly and then told me she wanted to have a threesome with none other than Desire."

"What the fuck?"

"Exactly, apparently Marie and Desire shared a kiss and decided to blame it on the alcohol, but my wife is definitely bi-curious. She went into a spill about how she knows I wanna fuck Desire and she is down with it as long as she can have her too."

"Man, I am having so much trouble making this make sense. Ok, Marie is telling you go ahead fuck Desire but she gotta be able to hit it too? Damn that's a pimp move. Are you sure we talking your Marie, the quiet, conservative, sometimes uptight Marie that turns her noise up at everything, Marie? This is hard to believe."

"Come on now, she's not that bad but yeah. My Marie has given me a free pass to fuck the woman who had my noise wide open as long, as she can partake, what luck."

Chase tried to act as if he was happy and excited for Hilton. He could see Hilton was overjoyed, but all he could think about was his Desire now becoming deeply involved with Hilton and then being with Marie. He had to admit that turned him on, but he couldn't just give them Desire, he had to make his move.

"So have you talked to Desire about this?"

"No, Marie told me she would handle it. All I know is she went over yesterday and came back and said it was a go. She was more excited than me. I decided I wasn't going to see Desire anymore alone. I realize we got too close and I love my wife so I can't get caught with my pants down alone with her, you feel me?"

"Yeah, I feel you, well Hilton, I got to tell you something." Chase was going to tell him the truth but he couldn't so instead he said, "Damn, I envy you."

Hilton took a sip of his drink and said, "I envy you with your freaky ass all out in public and shit. Let's talk about that."

"Haha, not today, I have an appointment I must get to. It's always good to see ya, hey keep me posted on your threesome. I wanna know all the details and make sure you take some Viagra or something hate for you to be limp at that party. One love bro."

"Love you too bro, I will get up with you soon."

As soon as Chase got in his car, he picked up his cell phone and dialed.

"Are you in your office? I'm on my way over, we need to talk." Chase sped off, he was furious and intrigued at the same damn time. He was not missing out on this.

MARIE

Guess he spoke with Hilton. Damn, men gossip just as much as women. I should have known he wasn't going to be able to keep the threesome quiet. Guess no man would be able to. I guess I need to deal with Chase before he screws something up.

Marie picked up the phone and dialed Nikki. She wanted to see if she could possibly come over after work and get it in. Since that day, Marie and Desire had fucked on several occasions. She'd become her muse. Marie knew she should be setting up the threesome but Desire's pussy was so good, she really didn't wanna share it. But she owed it to Hilton, so she was going to give it to him.

After the threesome she was just going to tell Hilton she was going to continue fucking Desire and he was going to have to deal with it. After all she didn't have to worry about Desire fucking Hilton or getting addicted. Desire had told her she was fucking Chase and she actually liked him, but she also enjoyed my pussy on her lips so I knew I wasn't going anywhere. However, Chase was a problem if he couldn't keep it together. He sounded like a loose cannon on the phone.

"Hey Nikki, are you going to be busy around 4pm? Let me know I need to get with you on our plans, call me." Marie said, hanging up the phone from leaving a message on Nikki's answering machine.

"So we doing a threesome, why didn't anyone inform me, what the fuck Marie, are you serious?" Chase said, as he entered Marie's office closing the door.

Without turning around Marie spoke, "Obviously you forgot who you are dealing with. Sit down!"

"I'm just saying..." Marie interrupted before Chase could finish, "You're just saying what, kneel!"

With those words, Chase dropped Marie's feet and began rubbing and kissing them.

"What do you need to say?" Marie commanded.

"I'm sorry Madame," bowing his head he continued, "Forgive me, do I get a spanking now, please spank me."

"No, you do not get rewarded for being rude, now what is your problem, get up back in the chair. Speak!"

Madame, I was just told by your husband, you and him and my Desire will be having a threesome and I am not involved."

"Of course you are not invited, it's a threesome. And you know what else; you don't get everything you want. Awe, are you upset? Poor baby, don't get mad, I have a special job for you on that night. You are going to record it, ok?"

"Yes Madame. And you know what, if you take beautiful videos, I will let you watch Desire and I fuck ok?"

"Yes Madame."

"And if you ever come at me like that again, I will take your balls. Understand?"

"Yes Madame."

"Now get the fuck out of my office, you disgust me."

Chase got up and left without saying another word. Marie laughed at the fact that she had total control over him. She tried her dominating skills on him accidentally and it worked and she took full advantage. Chase did everything she asked of him. She never asked for any sexual favors and he felt worthless because she didn't but he was fully aware that she had a hold on him and no matter what he did. He couldn't shake yearning to be dominated and Marie took full advantage of that. Marie had yelled at Chase one day and he responded in such a manner that showed her the power she have over him. She hardly ever used her power but when she did the results amazed even her. Maybe she had those powers over Desire and her husband. Guess the best way to find out is to try it.

Marie's phone rang distracting her from her day dream. "Hello." Marie said.

"Hey girl, it's me Nikki. Of course I have time for you come on by. How soon can you get here, 4pm seems like such a long time."

"I'm on my way."

"See you in a minute."

"Let yourself in."

Marie thought to herself, I know she thinks I am coming to fuck her, but I am bringing her over to my place, its time. The kids are with the grandparents, I want dick and I want pussy so it's going down tonight. Maybe I will get a sample taste before we leave.

...AND THEN THERE WERE THREE...

We turned on the music and served drinks. We struck up conversations about everything from movies to sports. It was the best night ever. We kept laughing and slamming back shots. The ladies danced closer and closer, then we drank, and the ladies danced, and we laughed, and the ladies danced closer, and closer, until they were gyrating on top of each other's legs, caressing each other softly but with determination. If Hilton didn't know any better, he would have thought they had done this before. The two of them were sharing such an intimate moment he found it very necessary to interrupt.

"Can I join in on this dance?" He asked, without waiting for a reply he stepped in between the two women and started dancing.

Marie suddenly grabbed his dick and pulled him closer to her, kissing him. Desire pressed against Hilton's back reaching through his legs grabbing his scrotum and the deeper and more passionate the kiss was between the two, the tighter she squeezed Hilton's sac, while thumbing the area between the anus and nuts. Neither one could keep their hands off one another. Hilton rubbed his wife's tits and she removed his hands and placed her fingers gently between Desire's legs where she could feel her soaked panties. All the while Desire stroked his g-spot and while he continued to tongue his wife down.

"Shall we move this into the bedroom?" Marie said as she led Desire by the hand who in turn led Hilton.

In the bedroom, Hilton was shocked to see Chase standing with a video camera.

"What are you doing here?" Hilton asked.

"He is with me, don't worry he isn't joining in, he is recording it for us." Marie said.

"Hilton, take of your clothes. Desire will take off my clothes and I will take off hers. Let's give Hilton a show. Are you ready?"

Marie ripped off Desire's shirt while she pulled her skirt up and off exposing a freshly waxed Brazilian pussy. Her titties flopped out and Marie saw her husband's face light up and his dick throbbing at attention. Hilton started stroking his dick as he watched the two of us get undressed.

Desire started moaning and began to nibbling on Hilton's neck while her lips parted and his fingers entered her wet hot pussy. Marie knew it was time and reached for Hilton's belt and grabbed his cock, which sprung out to stand at attention. Seeing it for the first time and no longer fantasizing about it Desire dropped to her knees and started to swallow Hilton whole. She was incredible. Somehow, she fit my entire thick member into and down her throat. What she was doing with her tongue almost made me want to explode right away. She licked from the balls to the shaft a few times teasing me. All the while she was looking at me with those eyes.

Then she dove in and went for the kill. Teasing my testicles she let me grab the back of her head and throat-fuck her. She loved the abuse. Hilton was forcing her faster and faster, until Desire couldn't take it. Breaking free she spun around and told me to fuck her as hard as I could. I looked at Marie, to make sure this was okay with her, and saw Desire begin consuming her pussy like it was her last meal. Chase walked closer towards us angling the camera like a professional. Kneeling behind her, Hilton grabbed her by the haunches and began to thrust; his long thick member penetrating deep into the folds of her hot, wet cunt. God! It felt so fucking incredible.

Desire rose up from Marie and let out a passionate moan, before she knocked the camera out of Chase's hand. Fumbling with his zipper, she ripped the button from his pants, pulling out his engorged dick and taunting the tip with her tongue.

Desire bucked and moaned. Just as she started to cry out above me in pleasure I pulled out and began to suck on her hard little clit, playing with it in my teeth and heightened the ecstasy of her orgasm. Cumming all over my face she collapsed on top of me, just in time to see Marie throw her head back in pleasure from Chase fisting her and Desire sucked him, his body tensed and he came all over their face. Desire grabbed his throbbing sloppy cock, lifting my wife and pressed it up inside her pussy. She was cuming all over it and I shoved my hardness back into Desire with force as the sounds of both women sent me to the edges of ecstasy and back.

We collapsed with a sigh of sheer sexual exhaustion and satisfaction. Sweaty skin lay on sweaty skin and everyone oozed of sex and happiness. The men barely had time to catch their breath before the ladies started a show of their own with us.

Marie grabbed Desire's by the hair and pulled her up in a sitting position on the floor. She told her to take her time and then she knelt down, spread her pussy lips and Desire started licking her cunt. She held my head firmly in place and started rocking back and forth. Desire grabbed her fleshy ass and started sucking that pussy. It seemed like it took forever, but finally she was moaning and gushing all in Desire's mouth.

Then she sat down on the bed, pulled Desire over to her lap and started spanking her- hard. It took me completely by surprise, so I started squirming and begging her to stop but Desire seemed to love it and Chase was begging to be next. They were so turned on, Marie allowed the two of them to get together and they fucked each other's brains out while Hilton and his wife made love.

EPILOGUE

The lovemaking fuck fest lasted well into the morning light. Even after years of not having sexual relations with his wife. Hilton never imagined he would experience the fetishes and fantasies Marie had hidden for years. Easing out to of the tangled web, Hilton stood above the bed. The day was breaking from night. He wasn't quite sure of how he felt about the entire scenario. He only knew that at this very moment, this second he was a riding on a cloud. His eyes drifted towards his wife as she lay with arms wrapped around Desire, who in turn lay in Chase's arms.

A small chuckle arose inside his chest at the vision of Marie commanding Chase around. That boy has some serious sexual fetishes. Hilton was pondering how long this would continue. He was very sure he wasn't into being dominated, however he could never deny granting Marie her every wish. So if being a dominatrix was what she wanted. He had no problem letting her, as long as he was involved it was a win win situation for everyone. He had his soul-mate back and his desires had been fulfilled. Turning around Hilton decided to take a shower and begin preparing breakfast before everyone awakened.

Turning on the shower, Hilton felt the arms of his yearning wrap around his waist. Making their way towards his chest, she asked, "Can I join you Big Daddy?"

Smiling to himself, Hilton turned around, lifting her in the air. Her legs encased his waist. He thought to himself, I definitely love this lifestyle. He stepped into the shower to get clean and dirty at the same damn time.

Thank you for your purchase!

Other works by LaRedeaux:

SWEET LOVE

'TIL DEATH

OoPs!

OUTSOURCED